Praise for Svetislav Basara

"*The Cyclist Conspiracy,* Svetislav Basara's second novel to be translated into English (expertly by Randall A. Major), is a dizzying, vertiginous ride in which the real is constantly at loggerheads with the unreal . . . [Basara's] inventiveness is a strength, indeed a talent."

—*World Literature Today*

"It's like *The Da Vinci Code*'s older, more perspicacious sibling."

—*The Barnes and Noble Review*

"Filled with mind-bending philosophical, psychological, and conspiracy theories, Basara manages to weave a tale that both confounds and delights." —*Foreword*

"Such a slippery cult makes for a slippery account, but then that's much of the fun of *The Cyclist Conspiracy*. From involvement in the World War I-starting assassination of Franz Ferdinand to Stalinist connections as well as activity much farther afield (as in Indian Dharamsala), and including everything from letters from and about members to some of their more theoretical writing (on 'The Madness of Architecture', for example) Basara spins a nice shadowy, loony, centuries-spanning conspiracy." —*The Complete Review*

"At once a rich philosophical tome and vision-altering spoof of the same, this 'meta-goulash' will interest readers of Jorge Luis Borges's *Labyrinths* and Flann O'Brien's *The Third Policeman*." —*Publishers Weekly*

"Basara has here defined the most fundamental and powerful of fictional engines—the self-observing observer, riddled by doubt."

—Daniel Soar, *LARB*

OTHER BOOKS BY SVETISLAV BASARA
IN ENGLISH TRANSLATION

Chinese Letter

The Cyclist Conspiracy

Fata Morgana

In Search of the Grail

Mongolian Travel Guide

The Rise and Fall of Parkinson's Disease

Svetislav Basara

Translated from the Serbian by Randall A. Major

Dalkey Archive Press
Dallas, TX / Rochester, NY

Deep Vellum | Dalkey Archive Press
3000 Commerce Street, Dallas, Texas 75226
www.dalkeyarchive.com

Deep Vellum is a 501c3 nonprofit literary arts organization founded in 2013 with the mission to bring the world into conversation through literature.

Originally published in Serbian as *Uspon i pad Parkinsonove bolesti* by Derta, Belgrade, Serbia, 2006.

First English edition, 2026

Support for this publication has been provided in part by grants from the Texas Commission on the Arts, the City of Dallas Office of Arts and Culture, and the Addy Foundation.

Translation of this title was supported by the Ministry of Culture of the Republic of Serbia.

Paperback ISBN: 978-1-62897-632-8 | Ebook ISBN: 978-1-62897-633-5

LIBRARY OF CONGRESS CATALOGING-IN-PUBLICATION DATA

Names: Basara, Svetislav, 1953- author | Major, Randall A. translator
Title: The rise and fall of Parkinson's disease / Svetislav Basara ;
translated from the Serbian by Randall A. Major.
Other titles: Uspon i pad parkinsonove bolesti. English
Description: First English edition. | Dallas, TX : Dalkey Archive Press, 2026.
Identifiers: LCCN 2025034304 (print) | LCCN 2025034305 (ebook) | ISBN 9781628976328 trade paperback | ISBN 9781628976335 ebook
Subjects: LCGFT: Novels | Fiction
Classification: LCC PG1419.12.A79 U8713 2026 (print) | LCC PG1419.12.A79 (ebook)
LC record available at https://lccn.loc.gov/2025034304
LC ebook record available at https://lccn.loc.gov/2025034305

Cover art and design by Daniel Benneworth-Gray
Interior design and typeset by KGT

PRINTED IN THE UNITED STATES OF AMERICA

Man is not an animal because he knows he is an animal,
but because he was born doomed to death, and knows
how to live while destroying, and building only that which kills.

Nikolai Fyodorov

PAVEL KUZMICH KASATKIN

MORBUS PARKINSONI

FOREWORD

Demyan Lavrentyevich Parkinson, the inventor of the horrible disease, died of exhaustion in 1947 under the alias of Nikolai Nikolayevich Kuznetsov, in a gulag on the River Kolyma. Under the hackneyed name Parkinson, he was to spend an entire forty-three turbulent cadaverous years, until *perestroika* and *glasnost* and the demise of the USSR; if the facts from the existing chronology and biography are to be believed, Demyan Lavrentyevich (now already rehabilitated) contributed profoundly to that demise. D. L. Parkinson was, indeed, rehabilitated along with hundreds of thousands of both real and fictitious internees, and his name—the home of his pustular being—was restored. His illness, however, fell into oblivion, barely scraping by in a humiliating status. It is still *morbus Parkinsoni*, more popularly known as parkinsonism, but its surviving contemporaries all agree—the symptoms and clinical picture have nothing to do with the original Parkinson's disease. This is not just a mutation of the illness itself, like tuberculosis, which constantly finds biochemical strategies to adapt to antibiotics; no, parkinsonism, which is incurable anyway, is now a profane collection of syndromes borrowed from several insignificant diseases that, taken together, mostly look like Alzheimer's. Modern parkinsonism is obviously a fake. However, why would one fake a disease? The same question bothered F. R. Voznesensky, a historian with access to the archives of the imperial Okhrana, the NKVD, the KGB, and Lubyanka. The only question is: where does one begin? The uninformed—though everyone is uninformed about this issue—are nowhere even close to imagining the enormity of those archives, not to mention the uncountable number of documents stored in them. (According to some accounts,[1] those archives contain a record of all roads, towns, villages, streets, houses, and people, and all their writings and conversations encompassing the last three centuries.)

In the archive, just the *Mitrofanovsk Department* itself (that is the small town where Parkinson was born) covers 617,849 square feet, with more than 459,789,490,567 documents. It's all there, nothing is hidden, but to put together a picture of an event, or to reconstruct the biography of a certain person, it would take decades of dedicated work. Voznesensky had no choice. He opted for the method of reading random documents. He relied on intuition. He used his sixth sense. When talking about Parkinson, that's the best way. For months, Voznesensky worked feverishly. And the first results appeared—a solidly documented biography of Parkinson to the age of ten. But there's nothing in it. At least nothing interesting. That kind of stuff can be read in the syrupy stories of Russian realist authors. Those stories, those soap operas before the soap operas, were actually models for teaching and raising Russian boys in those days. Voznesensky, a fanatic (as only a Russian can be) devotee of literature, came to a disheartening discovery: realism in Russian literature dismantled Russian reality, it destroyed the simplicity of the Russian soul, it began circulating the absurd idea of

1. See the text *Memories of Demyan Lavrentyevich,* by V. L. Mekdonaljd.

social justice; ultimately, Demyan Lavrentyevich thought so, too, as he wrote in one place, "After Dostoyevsky, instead of the variety and colorfulness of the Russian soul, all that was left were five psychological types of Russians: Stavrogin, Raskolnikov, Marmeladov, Lebeziatnikov, and Svidrigailov."

However, if nothing significant was happening in the basements of the archives, if the folder (later entitled *The Rise and Fall of Parkinson's Disease*) suffered from anorexia, at a hopeless distance from serious historical study in the private life of our historian, the first pathological changes would appear. One evening he arrived home and found his wife, Valentina Nikolayevna, naked, brushing her hair before the mirror, a common scene in Russian middle-class homes. However, something unusual quickly followed, something thoroughly disturbing for a psyche formed in a political system founded on materialism. To her husband's greeting, Valentina answered, speaking through her anus, "Zdravstvuj, daragoj!" After his initial shock, Voznesensky sought refuge in rationalization. He figured it was chronic fatigue. He attributed the whole thing to nervous exhaustion. A brief disturbance of perception. Our historian, however, didn't know (or didn't wish to know) one crucial thing: disturbances of perception do not exist. You see what you see, and you just have to take it the best way you know how. Already the next day, he was to tell everything to Eduard Mandarinov, the poet from whom we found out all of this, not so much from the need to unburden himself so much as he was hoping that Mandarinov would tell him "forget all that nonsense," which is what he did in a certain sense. "Look," Mandarinov said, "you spend your days reading the manuscripts of an egregious drunk. Do you think you can get away with that without consequences?"

Partially calmed, Voznesensky continued to dig through the

archive materials. But he learned much more about the internal organization and hidden meaning of the archive than about the subject of his research. He realized that the archive is not the collective memory of the world, but its collective oblivion. That the human community is like its component parts—people have a subconscious, imagination, and fantasies. That researching the archive is a sort of virus. Yet, he did make some progress. Actually, significant progress. He found a copy of the banned journal *New Life*, with Parkinson's article *The History of My Disease*. In the article, he found important references which, to an extent, narrowed his field of research. Voznesensky was excited. Excitement (and this is a rule) leads to despondency. That same evening, he found himself doing a truly, truly disturbing semi-conscious deed. He was sitting there, Voznesensky, watching television, tearing large pieces of newsprint from *Pravda*, putting them in his mouth, and savoring them. A truly discomfiting situation. The fact that Valentina Nikolayevna had spoken through her anus (and had since then occasionally talked in her sleep from the same orifice) could be attributed to the imperfection of perception. But no amount of fatigue, no such imperfection of perception could justify the undeniable fact that he was eating paper and that he was finding an almost spiritual satisfaction in it.

That night, Voznesensky did not sleep a wink.

Mandarinov calmed him down already the next day. "Fedya," the poet told him, "You're spending your life among pieces of paper, you're turning into paper. What's strange about it if, now and then, you tear off a piece and eat it? Anyway, we grew up in a system where the area known as *normal* was rather narrowly defined. You should expand your mind. Who knows what all the stuff people in the West eat. Self-consciousness is important. Eat whatever you feel like." Voznesensky must have thought, "Really, what's so bad about it if I eat paper. Paper is cellulose. It's like I'm eating cabbage." Whatever the case, but not without a certain amount of trepidation, Voznesensky continued his tortuous labor in the Archives. The abovementioned references led him to the *Dostoyevsky Department*, one of the largest in the Archives, the surface area of which is equal to that of Bulgaria. It's difficult to work there among the crazed hordes of literary historians, doctors, philosophers, Fools for Christ, idlers and, simply put, nutcases, who are parasites on the legacy of Fyodor Mikhailovich. But nothing could be done about that. So long as he confirmed incontrovertibly that the great writer's epilepsy was in fact masking Parkinson's disease, if he could only establish a connection between Parkinson and Dostoyevsky, that would be a first-class scholarly finding. Like everything else related to Dostoyevsky. The disturbing series of events, however, seemed to have no end. Voznesensky discovered something that no single Russian dared to ever uncover: Dostoyevsky not only did not suffer from parkinsonism, he also did *not* suffer from his infamous epilepsy; the occasional, not so frequent, "attacks" of *something* were the consequences of nervous exhaustion caused by long hours spent at the gambling tables, and could hardly be placed under the diagnosis of this inane, modern parkinsonism, which has nothing in common with real parkinsonism.

Our historian, Mandarinov testifies, was on the verge of despair. Why was he discovering things he did not want to know? That no one dared to discover? Why should he expose facts from the storehouse of forbidden books which will just be returned there in short order, even more forbidden and unavailable? And perhaps together with them, Voznesensky himself, remade in paper form. Transformed into an unreliable document. Voznesensky made the decision to abandon his cursed research, and to dedicate himself to more lucrative, socially acceptable business. For starters, he went off to rest at his dacha on the outskirts of Moscow. And for several days, he did indeed rest. But then, one morning, he was confronted with a truly, truly, truly disturbing event.

He woke up in the pigpen, among the swine. He had not been drunk the previous evening. Nor the one before that. Voznesensky, in fact, never (or almost never) drank.

It was true that the USSR had collapsed, it was true that the political system had changed and that the transition was ongoing, but essentially, in Russia, nothing ever really changes. Voznesensky was aware that he had gone rather far beyond the boundaries of *normal behavior,* beyond the narrow territory of reality whose borders had not been drawn by Russian revolutionaries but by Russian realist writers. He made an emergency appointment to see the psychiatrist. The psychiatrist, a typical *mechanic of the human soul,* educated in the Khrushchev era, did not know what to do with the available symptoms. —It seems to the patient that his wife speaks through her anus! Pffff! Women are constantly babbling. The words bounce off the walls. It is not always easy to determine where their words are coming from. —The patient is eating paper. Nothing terrible. People eat worse things: knives, razor blades, mortar, coal—he'd seen plenty of that in his practice. In any case, perhaps the patient's metabolism was lacking in lead or printer's ink. —The patient was sleeping with pigs. Big deal! The tough guy got drunk, but claims he never drinks. Same old story. Alcoholics are alcoholics because they don't admit they're alcoholics. All in all, the behavior is not so normal, but the psychiatrist knows more highly imbalanced people in key positions in the military and administration. Taking everything as a whole, he proclaimed his diagnosis, "You suffer from a mild form of hypochondria. I recommend that you don't rest. Idleness has a bad influence on your psyche."

Neither the psychiatrist nor the historian knew or, more precisely, did not wish to know, that hypochondria does not exist. That hypochondria, like paranoia, is always right. That the absence of an illness's manifestations in no way means that the person is not sick. That, ultimately, it is impossible not to be ill. That man himself is in fact an incurable disease.

Voznesensky went back to work. As he left the metro at Smolensk station, he thought he was being followed. But he ascribed that impression to his fatigue, and in the future would believe that no one was following him. The postulates of dialectical materialism are an effective sedative. Voznesensky was probably thinking something like, "I have enough problems with my hypochondria, I really don't need paranoia as well." In this, he was right. He had enough problems. He didn't need paranoia. But this was not paranoia at all. Voznesensky was indeed being followed. More precisely: I, Pavel Kuzmich Kasatkin, followed Voznesensky day and night on assignment from the Service which—as opposed to Parkinson's disease—prescribed the name but not the methods and essence as well. How else could I have written these lines? How else could I have learned so many intimate things about "Gobbler" (Voznesensky's operative name)? That's also quite logical. The archive is open, and it is available to scholars and researchers, but things must be kept under control. From the Archives, one must not take out, much less publish, a single letter more than the minimum necessary for constructing the democratic image of the country. (Maybe later I'll explain how it happened that I turned a deaf ear to the strict rules of the Service. That I betrayed it by making public the very thing I was supposed to stop. Perhaps I won't. I'm just a peripheral character in this story.)

Voznesensky went back to work. But the old fervor was gone. His enthusiasm. His élan. Maybe those people are right who say that one ought not to muck around in the past. Much less to make an attempt at correcting the injustices there. So that no one thinks that what happened to them was not deserved. It's quite possible that superficiality is man's destiny, that so-called profundity is an artificial creation of the imagination. In the end, perhaps we should trust Dostoyevsky's authority, who in one document (though of problematic authenticity) speaks about Parkinson and his family like this: "It is not to be excluded that the medical skills of the Parkinsons were based on personal experience, on the syphilis of Samuel Longfelovich, which, in ever worsening form, was passed from generation to generation, to the point where the disease reached its peak in the person of Demyan Lavrentyevich, in some ways the very incarnation of syphilis, where we are no longer dealing with a man carrying a disease, but with a disease that has become a man." "What can be done?" Voznesensky wondered. If he abandoned his research, he would never again be at peace. Valentina Nikolayevna would continue to speak through her anus. Perhaps through some other, even worse, location as well. Who knows what was waiting for him. There is, in any case, a critical point in any human endeavor, a point in which returning to the previous state is impossible. A point after which one must forge ahead regardless of the outcome. And Voznesensky went on clearing his path through the thick layers of archive material. Already three years deep in the Archive. From the clouds of paper dust, the contours of Demyan Lavrentyevich Parkinson begin to emerge. The picture is far from being clear. But it was certain: Parkinson knew, socialized, and corresponded with so many intelligent, important, and educated people that Dostoyevsky's claim that Demyan Lavrentyevich was "an alcoholic and syphilitic" simply did not stand. It was not in vain that he had hedged on such a possibility with his comment "the text is of problematic authenticity." (How cowardly scholars are!) "Who the hell was this Parkinson, and what kind of disease did he suffer from?" Voznesensky wrote in his journal in those days. Of course, he did not even imagine that his notebook was made of special holographic paper; he did not dream that everything he was writing appeared instantly in a journal-twin located in one of the Service's offices. The Service and psychiatry are interwoven, they complete each other, without psychiatry, at least in the lower ranks, being aware of it. It is a closed circle. One cannot go to the psychiatrist and say, "Doc, everything I write appears instantly in a journal-twin, and the agents of the Service read every word."

But thanks to that journal-twin impregnated with invisible holographic ink, I was able to reconstruct all the details of F. R. Voznesensky's research adventures. Otherwise, I wouldn't know what Voznesensky was thinking. What he was dreaming. This way, it is enough for me to leaf through the journal in the evening and find that on May 23, 1993, our historian dreamt of Jakob Böhme. "I have no idea what Jakob Böhme looked like, but I am certain it was him. Anyway, it was a nonsensical dream. Böhme was repairing some boots and constantly repeating, 'The soul, Voznesensky, the soul . . .'" In those days, Voznesensky didn't have much time for the soul. References, records, footnotes, marginal notes in books—all of that sent him to continue his research in the *Lenin Department*, whose surface area fits the territorial surface of the former USSR. Imagine all the documents there! What a wonderland! In the enormous catalogue of forbidden and confiscated texts about Vladimir Ilyich, Parkinson holds a place of honor. Approximately 99% of which no one would dare to even look at, much less research or publish. Voznesensky quite accidentally found a letter-twin (significant also for the history of the Service because this was a primitive version of holographic paper) in which it said, in Parkinson's barely legible handwriting:

> *Lenin is so loyal to the doctrine of materialism that he is slowly transforming into pure material.[2] Thanks to that he is as strong as iron. And his will is the same. Unless they find someone with a bullet or strong dose of poison to wound that organism, composed entirely of malignant cells, there is a danger that V. I. will live to be 350. Russia cannot allow this to happen for its own sake. The truth is, he will be cruelly punished for his misdeeds: after his death, he will be preserved like a wild boar[3] and exhibited for the commoners to look at, and his sinful soul—being tortured already right now by the devil—will observe that the entire scene for a long period of years.*

Voznesensky was in shock. The letter was addressed to Fanny Kaplan, the revolutionary who was to shoot Vladimir Ilyich Lenin one year later, in 1918. That was a first-class scholarly fact. Irrefutable evidence that Demyan Lavrentyevich Parkinson was the inspirer of the conspiracy against Vladimir Ilyich. It was just a shame that it could not be published. In spite of everything, Voznesensky went on with his research. He ignored the dubious ease of access to the

---

2. This proved to be true. In the autopsy record of V. I. Lenin, the renowned doctor V. Osipov notes among other things, "(. . .) the final diagnosis refutes the story of syphilis and arsenic poisoning. It was arteriosclerosis which completely encompassed the brain. The calcium deposits were so thick that, during the dissection, one could hear a sound like someone striking a rock."

3. As is well-known, this also proved to be true. Lenin was embalmed and exhibited on Red Square, where his soul to this day observes his corpse in a transparent casket.

official versions and documents; he researched texts on cigarette packages, notes on shirt cuffs, receipts, and bills. He went to the department of book-twins,[4] and there found the study entitled *Stalin*, which E. Radzinsky wrote as late as 1996. "In her written testimony," it says on page 161, "F. Kaplan said that she shot Lenin because she thought he was advancing socialism by several decades. When asked about co-conspirators and her party membership, Kaplan said that she carried out the assassination completely on her own. Malkov, the Kremlin's commandant, took Kaplan into the courtyard and shot her in the back of the head on September 3. The poet Demyan Bedny was an interested witness. Kaplan's body was set alight in a barrel."

Why did Voznesensky read a book that he knew to be a fabrication? Such questions are asked only by those who are not familiar with the secrets of Russian archives. Just as there is no perfect crime, there is no perfect fabrication. Every fabrication contains a certain percent of truth. One just moves from the fabrication toward authenticity. Our historian went to the Archive library, in the catalogue under *M* he found "Malkov, Apolonovich Vyacheslav," and then his book *The Russian Fasting Cookbook*; he opened it to page 161 and—instead of a recipe for borscht of beets and mushrooms—he found the authentic statement of Fanny Kaplan: *I wanted to kill the bastard who intended to heal Russia of a redemptive illness. That's all.*

Some things were now clearer to Voznesensky, although they would never be completely so. On the contrary, as time went by, everything became more obscure. D. L. Parkinson, Voznesensky discovered, was not a mere theoretician, a bookworm, but a man

4. Book-twins are similar to journal- and letter-twins. The difference is that book-twins are written by the Services. Usually, they are "written" again after several years.

of action. A counter-revolutionary! The leader of a secret society that almost changed the course of Russian history. Our historian decided, despite the dangers of such an undertaking, to expose to the light of day at least a tiny part of the saga of Parkinson and his disease. But he was hindered from doing so by a sudden illness. A strange enervation. Awful nausea. A high temperature that sometimes rose to 185 degrees Fahrenheit. This abnormal temperature was not the harbinger of ensuing death, but the fire of purification. The alchemical process *nigredo,* from which Voznesensky arose with the recognition that his life was at a crossroads, that, if he wished to plumb the mystery of Parkinson's biography and of parkinsonism, he himself had to contract Parkinson's disease.

Voznesensky decided to become ill.

"The state which we call 'health,'" he wrote that same evening in his journal-twin, which I was reading that very evening, "is actually a state of lethargy, lassitude caused by the absence of pain. The healthy organism is a kind of protein soup—the nutrient base for the creation of profane illness. I was relieved as soon as I got infected. Above all, parkinsonism is a disease that one accepts voluntarily. It is a matter of free choice. It is actually not a disease in the classical sense, but is indeed what John of the Cross calls 'the dark night of the soul': achieving consciousness of the poverty of biology and the metabolism, insight into the fallen state of the soul. As John of the Cross puts it, 'The divine light is always shining, but from the outset the soul can see only what is near to it or, better said, inside of it. That is: one's own darkness and depravity.' In these dark times of ours, Parkinson's disease is the most elevated form of godliness."

For Voznesensky, everything was now different.

What used to be easy became untenable. What used to be burdensome became lightness. To the general wonderment of his friends and family, without explanation, he divorced the gorgeous Valentina Nikolayevna and two days later married a certain Katarina, likewise a Nikolayevna, Bezuhovna, an indescribably ugly woman, missing a leg, who was a chronic alcoholic with an unbearable character, and he showered her with touching gentility and care. He turned a deaf ear to all the objections, chattering, and gossiping. In his life, from that moment forth, only two things were important: caring for Katarina Nikolayevna, patiently enduring her whims and insults, and his dedicated work in the Archives. The behavior of his second wife was indeed shameful. Crippled, hideous, intoxicated, she somehow managed to find a lover (the building custodian, a failed outpatient of the Voroshilova Mental Clinic), and openly cheated on Voznesensky. So shamelessly and openly that on several occasions I was tempted to liquidate them with my service revolver and set the whole thing up as if it were a showdown of the Chechen mafia. But I restrained myself, convinced that Voznesensky knew what he was doing. That there was some hidden meaning in the whole affair. And it turned out that I was right.

In the end, I would also be overcome. I was also to be infected. It would be a sort of work-related injury, because parkinsonism is passed on by reading stories about parkinsonism. But I will not, for understandable reasons, be able to receive the satisfaction of a health-related retirement.

Now, once Voznesensky was sick, Parkinson and parkinsonism revealed themselves to him like mirror images. The mystical abysses of the sacred illness opened before Voznesensky. It is a truly old disease. Demyan Lavrentyevich is not its discoverer; he is just one in a series, if I may say so, of the bodhisattvas of parkinsonism. Actually, the last one. He offered the world a saving disease, and the world chose deceitful and lethal health instead. Voznesensky found Parkinson's *Genealogical Tree of Great Valetudinarians,* whose founder was Job the Righteous. The Old Testament is filled with clinical pictures of Parkinson's disease. Let us randomly look at the Psalms of David; let us enjoy the blessed suffering. "The sorrows of hell compassed me about; the snares of death prevented me." (18:5) "For my life is spent with grief, and my years with sighing: my strength faileth because of mine iniquity, and my bones are consumed." (31:10) "My heart panteth, my strength faileth me: as for the light of mine eyes, it also is gone from me. My lovers and my friends stand aloof from my sore; and my kinsmen stand afar off." (38:10-11) And Nostradamus's prophecy, in the verses dedicated to events in the nineteenth century mention the riddle, "(. . .) the disease which will at the outset look like health, will be an illness unto death; and sacred health will appear, briefly, seeming like a disease; and there will be a battle in the world of the two illnesses, until the death of the king of the west and the king of the north. And mortal health will be victorious for a while. And the Antichrist will sit in the north."

F. R. Voznesensky's friends indeed left him. Every single one. One can hardly blame them. How does one be friends with a man who eats nothing but paper and more and more frequently sleeps in stalls and pigsties? How to befriend an eccentric married to a constantly-drunken, crippled, and mean-hearted woman? Our historian didn't give a red cent for any of that. Perhaps it is all unpleasant; it is important, however, that he is ethically correct; so that he fits in with the biblical text. Parkinson's disease is not like those banal human maladies limited to the area of a single human body. No! The sacred disease is of such a nature that it utilizes the pathology of external events and people in its advancement. But it also influences them. Parkinsonism is not passive; its manifestations often take on forms of political action. And not just political. Readers with a good memory will certainly recall the series of unexplained nocturnal terrorist attacks on football stadiums and gymnastic halls in the mid-1990s in Moscow, Tbilisi, and St. Petersburg. Each of them was blamed on the Chechens. In fact, those were the work of Fyodor Voznesensky. An expression of his righteous wrath toward the abhorrent shrines of godless health.

Even Demyan Lavrentyevich himself did not shy from occasional terrorist attacks. At the outset, especially among more educated people, parkinsonism was more popular than Marxism, socialism, and nationalism. But, as time went by, as a result of the progressive weakening of discipline in the masses, the seductive doctrines of satiety and health began marching toward a victorious defeat over humanity. There was no choice: the masses must be infected. Are there any better-suited circumstances for spreading an illness, an epidemic, and infection, than war? "History is," notes Demyan Lavrentyevich, "an insidious disease that not even parkinsonism can heal. Radical measures are necessary. A cosmic surgical operation. A world war that will remove the diseased tissues." The secret society *Parkinson's Little Brothers,* led by Demyan Lavrentyevich, worked conscientiously on creating the conditions for the outbreak of an all-encompassing global conflict. Parkinson was personally disgusted by bloodshed. But he knew that it was bad blood. That, let's say, if Fanny Kaplan had not, on orders from Demyan Lavrentyevich, shot Lenin and endangered his health, Vladimir Ilyich would have lived long enough, systematic and persistent as he was, to actualize the communist project of the ideal society. Everyone in Lenin's Utopia would have an apartment, a job, a bathroom, free medical care and education; the formula: eight hours of work, eight hours of culture and leisure, eight hours of rest, it would function perfectly. That would be a happy community. But for the human being there is nothing more lethal than happiness. The Sin of the East would become a part of the genetic code in a few generations.

And Voznesensky was aware of that. He did everything he could in his life to extinguish anything that even hinted at that ignoble feeling. Just as he unexpectedly got divorced and remarried, he just as unexpectedly quit his job as a collaborator at the Institute of Modern History, sold his luxurious apartment in Arbat for practically nothing, bought a peasant's house on the outskirts of Moscow, and opened a shoemaker's shop. He quit going to the Archive. Regardless, he was denied access there. But unnecessarily. He was now communicating directly with Demyan Lavrentyevich. Before he left his hovel outside Moscow forever and, who knows under what name and in what shape, departed in an undetermined direction, Voznesensky compiled a chrestomathy—a mixture of chronology, biography, and bibliography—in which he gathered the available documentation about Demyan Lavrentyevich (most of it of dubious origins) and the fragments of his writings from which a careful reader can reconstruct or at least get a hint at the contours of his doctrines. Thanks to the paper-twins, I came into possession of a copy of that manuscript. I am copying it and sending it to publishing houses in the fleeting hope that someone will dare to publish it, and in the even more fleeting hope that, in the grim era of post-parkinsonism, a few courageous people will be found, prepared to set off on the adventure of sacred illness.

The rest, no matter how they come into contact with this material, are not in danger, because even though parkinsonism is transmitted by reading, it is still a matter of free choice.

INFECTION

The sorrows of hell compassed me about,
the snares of death prevented me.
Psalms 18:5

For my life is spent with grief, and my years with sighing:
my strength faileth because of mine iniquity,
and my bones are consumed.
Psalms 31:10

1884. During an outing with his friends, Demyan Lavrentyevich Parkinson suddenly got an acute attack of a mysterious illness which would later be named after him—parkinsonism. The intensity of the attack and terrible pain were such a horrible sight that Parkinson's *friends fled in panic, not even attempting to come to his aid.*

Several years later, Demyan Lavrentyevich was to describe the course of the attack: "General weakness, trembling, diarrhea, vomiting, internal bleeding, a rash and purulent ulcers, high fever (even up to 180 degrees), extremely high blood pressure (350/220), insufficiency of the kidney, cardiac arrhythmia, muscle and bone pain, occasional blindness and deafness." He wrote further, "Torn apart by the most terrible pain, I still managed to muster the strength to realize my friends were unable to help me, and that medical science could do nothing. Because my illness is not of this world. I cried out, 'I admit my guilt, and I sorrow for my sins', and 'Do not forsake me, Lord, my God! And do not go far from me.' And that helped. The pain, fever, and external symptoms suddenly disappeared. Which did not mean that I was healed. No, the disease remained painlessly but powerfully inside me as an independent entity, like another me, which I allowed to develop and carefully studied the further changes. This research led me to the knowledge that medical science has a mistaken approach to disease; it is focused on health and not disease, which it considers to be a foreign, enemy body, some sort of parasitic organism. But I realized that illness is an inalienable, most sensible, and most creative part of life. Moreover, it is the path to healthiness. That illness is the most intimate part of each patient, the solution to his fate, and that there can be no place for the involvement of positivistic science and third parties, medical science and practitioners motivated by profit, who are not able to treat illness, but only to worsen it and cause the genesis of new, formerly unknown diseases."

1884. Demyan Lavrentyevich confessed to Zosima the Elder, who stayed briefly at the family dacha of the Parkinsons, in Mitrofanovsk. The great ecclesiastic encouraged Demyan Lavrentyevich to persevere. "It is the sacred disease," said Zosima. "You have come to know hellish suffering. You have come to know that the human body is left to itself, the sort of suffering life becomes when the Lord 'turns his head', that is, brother, when He withholds his help. Go, suffer, and be apart . . ."

1884. In secrecy, Parkinson headed to Tibet where, according to credible documents, he studied Buddhist medical texts until late autumn 1877. There are, however, equally credible if not more credible documents that indicate that he spent that period in Moscow, where he was a frequent and quite welcome guest at fashionable intellectual gatherings. Nothing strange in that. The time between

1845 and 1905 in historical science is known as "the black hole of chronology," a temporal period in which it is ultimately difficult to establish the order of events. On the other hand, in Parkinson's rather humble legacy, there is no record on which we could determine where he really was. That same year, in the journal *New Life,* his first article appeared (signed under the pseudonym of L. A. Sieri), *The Idea of Parkinson's Disease,* from which we learn that the father of Parkinson's disease is none other than Righteous Job. There follows a short history of the disease and the works of its famous sufferers, among whom—we shall mention only a few from the list of the 144,000 greats of parkinsonism—are the Old Testament prophets, King David, the Pharaoh Ramesses, Nero, Octavian Augustus, Plato, Socrates, Origen, St. Augustine, Charlemagne, St. Thérèse, Francis of Assisi, Charles the Hideous, Jakob Böhme, Marquis de Sade, Napoleon . . .

The article, overly fantastic, overly twisted even for the Russia of the time, amenable to the fantastic and twisted, caused wild polemics.

The Imperial Censors banned *New Life.*

Because of a political text. Parkinson mistakenly believed it was because of his *Idea.* The entire print run of *New Life* was confiscated and incinerated.

Parkinson was intensively thinking about the mystery of parkinsonism: why do the actions of a certain number of sufferers contribute to the benefit and health of mankind, while the activities of other famous patients make it worse and they become even more ill.

1887. Demyan Lavrentyevich solves the mystery behind the ambivalence of Parkinson's disease. Originally spiritual and purifying, the illness for some unknown reason mutates into a profane form—parkinsonism—which affects more base characters: ambitious people who are unable to withstand pain. But who are more than able to inflict it. The profanation of illness is the basic reason for the sudden rise of medical science, the later industrialization of healing, and the development of techniques for the seeming removal of pain. Because "pain relief," Parkinson notes, "certainly does not mean curing the illness. On the contrary! Disease is most dangerous when it doesn't hurt."

Parkinson's later research uncovered one more, absolutely desacralized, mutation: parkinsonism C, the final stage, in which the illness has so advanced that it seems to be health. Indeed, the clinical picture at that stage leads down the wrong path: pulse, blood pressure, blood workup—all in normal limits; general state—good. (Approximately 75% of the world population suffers from parkinsonism C; most people, however, are not conscious of their illness till the moment of death.)

Despite the absence of clinical symptoms, the disease is easily recognizable on the basis of pathological changes in behavior. Sufferers usually go running in parks for no reason; they clamber up inaccessible mountain peaks; they intentionally jump into the water and swim around aimlessly; they visit gyms; they don't drink; they don't smoke, and they pay attention to their nutrition.

In an extensive letter to the Imperial Duma, Parkinson pointed out the need for far-reaching reforms. 1. Renaming the Ministry of Health to the Ministry of Illness. (A reasonable suggestion: health is not the problem, the problems of illness and the unwell need to be solved.) 2. Conjoining the Medical Faculty with the Theological Faculty "(. . .) in order to inhibit the further despiritualization and desacralization of medicine." The letter never reached the Duma. Hundreds of crazy, impulsive, and impossible letters arrive there every day. In the Duma, there is a special department where the clerks read letters and assign them to other departments.

Parkinson's letter ended up in the *Fools for Christ Department.*

1888. Parkinson departed again for Tibet. This time—a rarity in those days—all the available documents agree. We even have Parkinson's notes, a kind of journal, from which we learn that the subject of his research was not the study of Buddhist medical books, but the investigation of palingenesis, in the West mistakenly called "the migration of souls." Demyan Lavrentyevich, of course, did not believe in the migration of souls, nor even in the incarnation of certain energy entities based on karma; he was an orthodox Christian. His interest in palingenesis is not related to the otherworldly. Palingenesis interested him as a technique of changing one's identity in this earthly life. The mystical knowledge he gained in Tibet was to serve him well in the upcoming years as an effective protection against the incessant persecution of the secret services. After his second visit to Tibet, Parkinson began to proliferate, a series of metamorphoses and changes of his outward appearance ensued, although—R. D. Meyerhold claims—his real identity remained unchanged the whole time under thick layers of illusory personal descriptions.

Upon returning from Tibet, because of serious frostbite, he spent three weeks in the *guberniya* hospital in Irkutsk. Recovering to a certain extent, he organized a rebellion among the patients. At the head of a column of lame, crippled, and exhausted patients, he went before the hospital administration with a demand for improving conditions and for a more humane relationship toward the patients. In order to convince them of the justice in their demands, he forced the administrators, doctors, and personnel to lie in the hospital beds, to eat the hospital food, and to undergo therapy.

"An incidental, but truly important experiment," he would write later in his notebook. "After just two days, formerly healthy as horses, the doctors and nurses all became ill, moreover, with the very diseases of the patients whose beds they slept in. Key proof of the thesis that hospitals, by manipulating certain symptoms, actually produce illnesses."

The patient rebellion, the first of three led by Parkinson, was quashed in blood. At dawn on the third day of the uprising, a unit of Cossacks galloped into the rooms and dormitories; the drunken Cossacks, as testified by the survivors, randomly shot people with their *Nagants* and mercilessly hacked away with their sabers. The balance of the hospital Thermidor: 57 dead, 194 wounded, 73 missing patients. The other side also recorded losses. Because of the sudden and forcible infection, 14 doctors and 28 nurses died. The Cossacks were not spared either. One *praporshchik,* thinking that a bottle contained spirits, drank a liter and a half of hydrochloric acid and died.

Five others mistakenly drank a dozen liters of methyl alcohol and went blind.

The surviving staff caught the apparent Demyan Lavrentyevich. They shaved his head. Filled him with castor oil. Put leeches on him. In the end, they tarred and feathered him. They didn't even notice that it was not Parkinson, but a random patient. Or maybe just a random passerby . . .

The real Parkinson was far away.

September: The mesmerist and alchemist Khalakhurov arrives in Mitrofanovsk.

October: The first sojourn of F. M. Dostoyevsky in Mitrofanovsk.

December: From who knows where, Lu Salome appears in Mitrofanovsk. Supposedly to celebrate New Year. In fact, the apocryphists claim, she came to steal Demyan Lavrentyevich's soul.

That New Year's celebration was to last four months and grow into a legend which would long after, spiced with fantastic aggrandizements, be recounted in the salons of Moscow and St. Petersburg, to the point that in the remote provincial corners it grew into a phantasmagoric *sotie*, most likely the closest to the truth about what happened in the cursed dacha of the Parkinson family. Demyan Lavrentyevich is terse when talking about the event. "Who could possibly know what happened. It lasted, that part is true, four full months, but everyone lost their minds already on January 1." In one of his letters, Semyon Frank quoted Parkinson's lapidary sentence about Lu Salome, "Over the three months I spent in the company of that enchantress, I found out more about hell than if I had spent thirty years in a cave in the Sinai Desert." On the only preserved page of Parkinson's infamous journal, a fragment was later found of his text about the sojourn of Lu Salome:

> *Another powerful episode of the disease. At this stage, the disease has a body; it is none other than the adventurist and suffragette Lu Salome. This attack will be harsher, but it will simultaneously allow more objective insight into the tangled ways of parkinsonism's pathology. The manifestations of the disease that are developing within* **my own** *body are too subjective; only when we confront the illness in someone else do we gain insight into the depths of our own rottenness. Lu Salome came to Mitrofanovsk without my invitation, probably without anyone's, but she was there quite legitimately, drawn by my shameful propensities and urges, which she was prepared to satisfy. Only to take my soul in return. In the niche that she happily showed the gamblers and debauchees at the dacha, she already had twenty-odd miniature crystal-beaded dishes*

where she kept the souls of her victims. With special pride, she showed the vial holding the soul of German philosopher Friedrich Nietzsche, who, in the end, had been only a vegetative shell. There's no doubt: Lu Salome is the woman-disease I read about in the writings of Jakob Böhme. All the cells in her organism are malignant. She does not know it, though. And she is thus as healthy as a horse. She is in fact a kind of psychophysical vampire, who constantly sucks in health, energy, money, jewelry, food, and drink. I despise such people, and yet Lu irresistibly attracts me and magnifies her allure to the point of frenzy with her absolute lack of interest in me. About which she is not pretending. Lu came to Mitrofanovsk drawn by the rumors of the production of enormous amounts of gold, and about my father's legendary munificence.

A person actually longs to be ill so as not to face the sins caused by the disease.

1888. Parkinson began his work on the essay *Tractatus antiheliocentricus.* This was to be a tumultuous year for our hero. A year of fateful encounters. Demyan Lavrentyevich set off on a pilgrimage to Yasnaya Polyana. Lavrentiy Akakyevich did not have (or, rather, did not want to have) money for the trip. As a fanatical admirer of Dostoyevsky and the informal priest of his cult, he did not have a high opinion of Tolstoy. Despite the fact that Tolstoy had mentioned him in one of his stories.

Demyan Lavrentyevich had a problem—Yasnaya Polyana was far away. How could he get there? But Demyan Lavrentyevich was resourceful; he would get there and along the way present the world with another discovery—hitchhiking—unintentionally paving the way for a future global sub-cultural phenomenon. Before he set off on his long journey, stopping carriage drivers, riding in drays full of manure, hiding in cargo wagons, Russia and the rest of the world had been mulling about in a sort of travel paralysis. If one did not have money for a stagecoach or the train, one did not travel.

The discovery of hitchhiking, however, proved to be the only positive outcome of the trip. Things in Yasnaya Polyana were completely unclear to Parkinson. The real Tolstoy was completely different from the representations of him stored in the fantasies of his admirers. Lev Nikolayevich gladly accepted visitors, but he expected them to observe him through the idealistic optics of those representations. He expected Parkinson to not be an exception. He could not even imagine the existence of exceptions. But Parkinson was one. He saw that Tolstoy was just one more in a whole series of Russian writers. To be fair, somewhat better than Dostoyevsky in terms of literary skill, but still just another Russian writer. Parkinson did not question his talent. Far from it. All that would change when Tolstoy accepted the redeeming illness, Parkinson hoped; Lev Nikolayevich would be able to shape it into literature and make it attractive; thousands of his fans would become ill, and Parkinson's disease would become fashionable . . .

"I have come to infect you with Parkinson's disease!" Demyan Lavrentyevich announced to "the Giant from Yasnaya Polyana." The Giant, however, turned out to be a dwarf. Tolstoy (though Parkinson did not know it) was a hypochondriac, frenetically afraid of pain, suffering, and death. "Help!" cried the great writer. "Help! This guy's infectious!" And, what happened? The custodians, servants, maids, visitors—that whole colorful crowd that hangs around Russian manors (and was masterfully depicted by Chekhov and Ivan Bunin)—surrounded Demyan Lavrentyevich. They sprayed him with primitive disinfectants. Then they beat him with rake handles. In the end, they smeared him with tar and poured feathers on him . . .

Parkinson took all of that calmly. He accepted it all as an external manifestation of the illness. As one more discovery about the mystical nature of parkinsonism and the basic impotence of medicine. Because, even if he had avoided being tarred and feathered as the leader of the rebellion in that hospital, the tar and feathers were waiting for him in the place where he expected to find the pathway to health.

His return to Mitrofanovsk was quite different from his departure. Namely, in the village tavern, Parkinson sold a rather large clod of earth, the property of Count Tolstoy, to a vagrant who wanted to be near Tolstoy. Now, Parkinson was traveling like a gentleman. First class. His conscience clear. The great writer had argued for the abolition of private property; let him see how that works out in practice. As Parkinson's train disappears around a bend, we can see the results of that for a moment. Tolstoy is beyond himself. He's crying out again. The custodians, servants, and maids grab the unfortunate buyer. They beat him with rake handles. They smear him with tar. They pour feathers on him . . .

The development of events is a matter of a different chronology, and it is of no interest to us any longer.

In his dreams, Jakob Böhme appears to Parkinson several times. "Those are not ordinary dreams," Demyan Lavrentyevich makes note. "I could touch the great mystic. Smell his breath." Parkinson himself identified that series of dreams as a turning point in his spiritual development. He remained terse. He says nothing of the content of their conversations, except that Böhme recommended that he read his writings, and entrusted him with the task of writing his biography. Parallel with the writing of *The Ideology of Heliocentrism,*

Parkinson began working on the manuscript of *The Final Days and Death of Jakob Böhme.*

Rasputin arrived in Mitrofanovsk.

The Final Days and Death of Jakob Böhme came out in print. The rather thin booklet attracted enormous attention by the literary public. The first edition of the 5,000-copy print run sold out in just two days. Several repeat editions followed. The Holy Synod of the Russian Orthodox Church accused Parkinson of spreading heresies.

Parkinson paid no attention to the accusation. Still, just in case, he left Moscow and headed off in an unknown direction.

1889. The third, worst attack of parkinsonism caused by Rasputin's sinister presence. "If the illness does not turn into a chronic form," Demyan Lavrentyevich confided in his friend Semyon Frank, "I will not survive the next attack." From the story that Frank told to Count Trubetskoy, who repeated it to Berdyaev, a horrible anamnesis arose: the attack was so powerful that it caused Parkinson's body to split into a healthy part and a sick one. To make matters worse, Demyan Lavrentyevich somehow observed the process of dissociation "from somewhere above." And he saw an astonishing sight: the half of his body from which the twin-sickness was separated, so the one that was considered to be healthy, had no life in it whatsoever. It was, in fact, Parkinson's future cadaver. On the other hand, the subtle structure of the sick half, which we observe only when it is in contact with "healthy" tissue, was shining with a gentle unearthly light. Now things were a little more evident: pain, all the unpleasantries of sickness in general, have nothing to do with illness. That which hurts is the mortal, perishable, biological part.

Parkinsonism set off on a victorious campaign. Under the influence of the text *The Final Days and Death of Jakob Böhme,* a religious sect of paper-eaters appeared in Moscow. From the outset, most of its followers were shoemakers. The leader of the sect, or perhaps it is better to use the modern word *guru*, a certain Vsevolod Lavrentyevich Mekdonaljd, was also a shoemaker. After reading the manuscript and learning that Jakob Böhme was a shoemaker by profession, Mekdonaljd, quite in the Russian spirit, was exalted, established a shoemakers' guild for the chosen people, and laid out the foundations for a grotesque cobbling messianism and an even more grotesque, completely minimalist theology and soteriology: be filthy, marry an ugly and evil woman, bear pain with patience, take communion made of paper, and you are saved. Berdyaev is right when he claims that the Russians tightly connect messianism with laziness, with their impatience for the arrival of the New Jerusalem where there will be no work. The Russians, moreover, are prepared to accept the wildest of ideas just to enjoy their leisure. Thus, the paper-eaters, with Mekdonaljd at the lead, threw their hands up from their work, closed their shops, sitting all day long in taverns, drinking vodka and dedicating themselves to theological debates. Winter was coming, and no valenki or boots were anywhere to be found. And not just in Moscow. The heresy spread like lightning across Russia. The Imperial government, merciless toward socialist and anarchist circles, for some reason was irrationally tolerant of heretical sects. Even though the latter were incomparably more subversive. After all, it was not Lenin who brought down the empire, but barehanded Rasputin.

And what are Bolshevism and the dictatorship of the proletariat other than Mekdonaljd's theology, from which every speck of spirituality has been removed?

Instead of taking a knout and forcing the shoemakers to grab their shanks and glue, the authorities invested money in the training of a new generation of shoemaker-atheists. A vain affair. They would make a couple of pairs of boots, inhale a bunch of glue, and immediately join the paper-eaters. Or the revolutionaries-anarchists. Things went too far. The Okhrana, not without a certain justification, suspected that Vsevolod Mekdonaljd was in fact Demyan Parkinson in disguise. But how could they prove it? And even more unpleasant, if that did happen after all, how could they avoid the inevitable rebellion of the paper-eaters who would—the Okhrana knew this—only be a spark for a general uprising of an enormous army of malingerers?

The Holy Synod of the Russian Orthodox Church believed it had a solution. The paper-eaters were to be drawn beneath the skirts of canonical Orthodoxy, under which there were already a plethora of pagan and telluric cults. In that way, the bishops believed, the heresy would be Christianized. Russian religious thinkers, themselves heretics to a man, were of a different opinion: that those cults, taken into the Church, were in fact paganizing Christianity.

The Patriarch of the Russian Orthodox Church invited Mekdonaljd to lunch. Mekdonaljd went to the Patriarch's Palace. He had nothing against Orthodoxy, he often attended church; under the influence of Böhme's Protestantism, he believed that his heresy was one of the countless ways which lead to the Heavenly Jerusalem. The conversation between the Patriarch and the Heresiarch took place in a benevolent atmosphere.

But Mekdonaljd refused to renounce his doctrines.

The imperial authorities made another in a series of mistakes that cleared the path to the October Revolution: they arrested Mekdonaljd and his followers and sentenced them to exile in Siberia. Till then localized to the region of Moscow, the paper-eater heresy spread to the east. As an irony of fate, or simple clerical idiocy—our heretics were assigned to work in a paper mill. Seventy-five percent of their production ended up as the sacrament in their obscure rituals. In the capital and large cities, there was a dearth of office paper, which slowed down the work of an already sluggish administration, thereby accelerating the revolutionary processes.

The heresy spread to Mongolia, China, and Persia.

The texts of Demyan Lavrentyevich were translated into foreign languages and published in the West.

The idea of parkinsonism slowly began to gather followers all over Europe. In Paris, London, Prague, and Berlin, *Secret Societies of Sacred Valetudinarians* began to sprout.

Members of the Parisian lodge—Villiers de l'Isle-Adam, Paul Verlaine, Joséphin Péladan, and Charles Baudelaire—turn the ideology of parkinsonism into poetry. The eyes of the entire artistic world were turned to Paris. Parkinsonism under a pseudonym—decadence—became mondain.

The first persecutions. The authorities of Prussia and Brandenburg outlawed the Society for the Study of Parkinson's Disease. Nazism was on the rise, although no one knew it, nor did it yet have a name, ideology, leadership, or armed forces. The presidents of both societies were sentenced to death and hanged. The membership was sent into prolonged imprisonment.

Parkinsonism conquered southeastern Europe as well. In the capital of the Kingdom of Serbia, a lodge under the name of the Black Hand was founded in a suburban café.

The police raided the dacha in Mitrofanovsk; they arrested Parkinson's father and with an expedited process sentenced him to banishment in Siberia. Lavrentiy Akakyevich Parkinson—a man ruined by his fanatical love of Dostoyevsky—was the connective tissue of the fragile micro-universe of vice in Mitrofanovsk; his willpower too long held together all the impossible spaces, ethereal structures, and absurd economy of the dacha. It all collapsed upon his departure. Through no fault of its own, the little town of Mitrofanovsk vanished from the face of the earth, along with half of the *guberniya*. The landlords whose property he sold, in the style of those times, generously forgave Lavrentiy Akakyevich's debts. They corresponded with the courts. Paid lawyers. In vain. Parkinson the elder had to go to Siberia.

The tortuous farewell scene at the Kiev train station was even attended by Fyodor Mikhailovich Dostoyevsky. In the line of the prisoners, the great writer noticed Parkinson. He took out his notebook. Semyon Frank (who also gladly watched such scenes but for completely different reasons) stood on his tiptoes behind the back of Fyodor Mikhailovich. He peeked into the notebook. Dostoyevsky was writing. "In the line of prisoners, L. A. Parkinson was also present, the former landowner who drank away his own property, and that of several neighbors."

After several moments, Dostoyevsky scratched out the sentence.

1890. Demyan Lavrentyevich left for Turkey. An empire on its deathbed, sicker than Russia, it would later prove to be fertile soil for the spread of his ideas. Turkey was so sick that there was plenty to learn from it. For the next few years, our hero was a hotelier. In the Laleli quarter, he ran the *Karadeniz Pansiyon,* which is indeed a hotel, but also a sort of hospital. The boarders were mostly tubercular Russian countesses, exhausted by their unhappy love affairs, who spent their final days there. We don't know much about that period in Parkinson's life. Almost nothing except that he introduced himself as İsmail Ağa Çengi, and that he spent his nights writing his capital work *Tractatus antiheliocentricus*.

Some events, however, indicate that Parkinson went to Russia incognito. It would be a stretch, for example, to ascribe the

September revolution in the largest Moscow hospital (the forerunner to the October Revolution) which almost destroyed the imperial regime to a spontaneous revolt of the sickest, most infirm patients. It is impossible that Parkinson wasn't involved. It all began, like back in Novosibirsk, seemingly harmlessly. The patients refused to eat breakfast and began to bang their spoons on their trays. A normal thing. Hospital food is bad. A few male nurses with nightsticks would be enough to put things in order. But not this time. The rebellion was well-organized, the discipline among the rebels ironclad. It all took place as if the rebels were following instructions from Malaparte's yet unwritten *Coup d'État, the Technique of Revolution*. They occupied the kitchen, pantry, dispensary, and operating rooms. They called a press conference for foreign and domestic correspondents. They appealed to the patients of other hospitals, polyclinics, and sanatoriums to join in the revolution. The response was beyond all expectations. Moscow's healthcare was completely paralyzed.

The lower-ranking personnel—nurses, cooks, cleaning ladies—stood with the revolutionaries.

On the list of demands, we can recognize Parkinson's handwriting: 1. equal rights for the healthy and the ill; 2. an end to the limited movements of patients; 3. the right of patients to establish their own diagnoses and determine their own therapies; 4. twenty representative seats for patients in the future Russian parliament . . .

Parkinson—now it was clear that he was the leader—was using the rebellion to lay the groundwork for a future Republic of Valetudinarians. According to the testimonies of the surviving participants, Parkinson's short-lived republic was organized on the principle of castes. Affairs of state were run by those suffering from primary parkinsonism, executive authority was relegated to those with parkinsonism B, while those with parkinsonism C dealt with oversight and the distribution of goods. All the rest, both the healthy and the slightly ill, were left with the hard and dirty jobs. This was not, however, because of racism, as certain western writers speculate; the caste division was prophylactic, meant to halt the further mutation of Parkinson's disease.

Set in the deceptive distances of Siberia, more of an urban plan than a city, Novosibirsk had been a suitable place for the attack of Cossack forces. But in Moscow, in front of the ambassadors, journalists, and world travelers, it was absolutely impossible to send in the army to battle barehanded patients, not even if they were threatening the societal order. One had to resort to more clever means. The authorities agreed to all the rebels' demands. Parkinson was wary. But the others were not. Their ideals began to fade quickly before the couple of sausages that the Ministry of Health promised as a replacement for the tasteless mush. The patients obediently returned to their beds. They waited for their portions of borscht and sausage. The deputy minister of health, in front of an entourage of ambassadors, and journalists, domestic and foreign, personally dished out the borscht and divvied up the sausages. And it was all over. Already the next morning, mush was again served on the trays. A few of the braver patients began to bang with their spoons. But there was no one left who could politicize the noise. Parkinson had taken his history of disease and departed.

Male nurses with heavy nightsticks entered the patients' rooms.

The *Tractatus antiheliocentricus* came out in Germany, under the penname *Michael Sendivogius,* a seventeenth century alchemist, a sworn opponent of Nicolaus Copernicus.

That same year, the *Tractatus antiheliocentricus* was translated into English, French, Swedish, and Spanish.

Jacob Burckhardt, who liked the *Tractatus,* noticed the sentence "the revolutionary replacement of the geocentric model with the heliocentric was the original form of the French Revolution and all the revolutions that would come out of it," on the basis of which he concluded that Sendivogius could not have been the author of the *Tractatus,* for the simple reason that he had died many years before the fall of the Bastille.

Burckhardt notes, "The real author of the *Tractatus,* judging by all things, was Demyan Lavrentyevich Parkinson."

Vsevolod Lavrentyevich Mekdonaljd accidentally fell into a woodchipper and was turned into a sheaf of the finest paper. His tortuous death and symbolic transmutation into paper insured him a saintly status.

1891–1900. Parkinson again headed off to Tibet where, in a state of deep meditation without food and water, he would spend an entire ten years. Parkinsonism victoriously spread across Europe. The better, nobler, and more educated part of the Old World entirely accepted Demyan Lavrentyevich's doctrine. Refined minds were able to comprehend that health is uncertain, temporary, deceptive, that illness is unavoidable and—since it is common to everyone—universal, and that good health pours oil on the already raging fire of selfishness and arrogance in the world. But, parallel with the flourishing of parkinsonism, barely hidden solar cults also begin to strengthen; the doctrines of strength, light, and health are incomparably more acceptable for the meandering masses and the lumpenproletariat amenable to self-deception. What is, for example, the opus of Richard Wagner other than Nazism in the form of music?

What are the other phenomena of introducing universal suffrage, shortened working hours, and the emancipation of women, other than communism?

1901. The secret Congress International of Parkinsonism in Bern. Demyan Lavrentyevich gave a speech in which he analyzed the situation in the world. The discreteness of the Congress, for understandable reasons as we will see, meant the absence of written documents. But absolute secrecy does not exist. Among the Congress participants, there was a rather large number of those suffering from parkinsonism C, the mutation characterized, among other things, by increased garrulity. If the rumors of those pariahs of parkinsonism are to be believed, the Congress participants concluded unanimously that the health situation in the world was alarming, that humankind was as a whole cleaner and healthier, that—due to that profane health—spirituality was weakening, and that the only salvation from the transformation of mankind into a colony of multicell organisms was the instigation of a world war. "Mens sana in corpore sano!" Parkinson thundered from a partially illegible stenographic transcript by one of the Congress members. "That pagan parole became state policy at the beginning of the twentieth century. The truth is different: the soul cannot be healthy in a healthy and fit body. Moreover, in such a body there can be no soul at all. The fact is that we feel better when, let me say it thusly, we are healthy, but the pleasantness of that feeling lowers the bar. Intoxicated by that feeling, people who used to be serious allow themselves to behave intolerably. Not a year goes by that they don't come up with a new sport of some kind, as if the existing athletic disciplines inherited from ancient pagan times are not enough. Look at how the cream of the English aristocracy is chasing balls around. For us to hinder the healing of the world, its transformation into a worthless biological mass, we, gentlemen, must instigate a world war. Only war, as the most edified form of parkinsonism, with its horrors and shedding of excess blood, can convince dullard humankind that it is sick."

The heads of the lodges were given the confidential Action Plan for Causing a World War.

Not a single copy of that plan has ever been found.

1902. Parkinson went to America. The immigration authorities forbade him, without explanation, entry into the territory of the United States. Demyan Lavrentyevich was forced to spend several months in quarantine, and returned to Europe on the steamship *Lusitania*. America will never recover from that, whether accidental or intentional, forbiddance. The cult of health, youth, nutrition, and sports, which unavoidably ends in idiocy, is stronger in America than anywhere else.

Lavrentiy Akakyevich Parkinson died in exile.

1902. Parkinson joined the Ottoman army as a sanitation officer and was assigned to the battalion commanded by the ambitious Major Kemal Paşa. In the years to follow, the two of them would transform the face of Turkey, although the fame for that undertaking would be claimed by Kemal Paşa—later Atatürk—for himself. If those two sufferers had never met, world history would certainly have taken on a different course. The "Patient from the Bosporus," as the western press called the Ottoman Empire at the time, was indeed an empire of sickness, a society in the advanced stages of disintegration, the most decadent country in the world. Even though the concept of "decadence" had not yet entered the Turkish language. If that was the Turkish language at all. Borrowings from Arabic and Persian, in more recent times French as well, had replaced Turkish words; everything indicates the unavoidable splitting of Turkish into dialects of Arabic and Persian, and thereafter the partition of Turkish territory into Persian and Arabic regions. Kemal Paşa saw where all that was leading. He was aware of the geopolitical catastrophe that would come about with the disappearance of Turkey as a Mongolian buffer-zone between the murderous fighting of the Aryan and Semitic worlds. But he did not know what to do. Until Providence sent him Demyan Lavrentyevich. Who knew quite well what to do. During just a few conversations beside campfires in the Anatolian wilderness, Demyan Lavrentyevich convinced Kemal Paşa that the de-Arabization of Turkish, the de-Arabization of Turkey as a whole, would be impossible as long as the Arabic alphabet was being used. Which was quite logical. He suggested the introduction of the Russian variation of Cyrillic as the most suitable for the phonetics of the Turkish language. Kemal Paşa was cautious. If the use of the Arabic alphabet had brought Turkish to the brink of disappearing, and the Turks a step away from assimilation, the introduction of Russian Cyrillic, an incomparably more aggressive alphabet, would quite quickly result in the Russification of all and everything, and the transformation of Turkey into a Russian *guberniya*.

A compromise solution would be the introduction of the Latin alphabet. On the spot, Lavrentyevich composed the future alphabet of Turkish. Over the next few days, Kemal Paşa busily learned to write. In Demyan Lavrentyevich's legacy, a piece of paper from an officer's notebook has been found, with the first word "Sovezluk," which Kemal Paşa, the Turk of all Turks, wrote in the new alphabet.

The next step toward Europeanization was a change in national fashion. Kemal Paşa was skeptical. He did not want to listen to Parkinson's suggestions. He did not understand why it was necessary to forbid the fez, feredza, and baggy pants. "What will remain of the Turks then?" he asked. "And why should we change our clothing anyway?" Demyan Lavrentyevich thought for a moment or two and said, "Kemal Paşa, can you imagine the following scene: seven men dressed in topcoats, wearing high-hats, impaling some poor soul?" Kemal Paşa tried to imagine such a scene. And he could not. "You're right!" he said. "I will forbid the fez and feredza, and impaling. In European Turkey, execution is to be carried out in a civilized way, by hanging or shooting."

This was the first larger action in the preparation for a purifying world war: the coup d'état of the *Black Hand* in Belgrade. King Aleksandar, who was leading pro-Austrian policy, was killed together with Queen Draga. The conspirators brought the pro-Russian Karadjordjevich dynasty to the throne. King Petar I Karadjordjevich, who was schooled in Russia, was a personal acquaintance of Demyan Lavrentyevich and a great fan of his writings.

The loudest criticism of the overthrow and regicide in Serbia came from England, the land of hunting, sport, and leisure activity. In the decades to follow, England would not miss a single chance to take revenge on Serbia and the Serbs.

The journal *New Life,* in its September edition, published the intimate writings of Demyan Lavrentyevich under the title "The History of My Disease," a visionary text which foresaw the short-lived rise and fall of parkinsonism. The Imperial censors banned *New Life.* This time, because of Parkinson's text. In the explication of the censors, it says, "For slandering Fyodor Mikhailovich Dostoyevsky, diplomatic scandals, and insults to public morality."

Thanks to the fact that twenty-odd copies of *New Life* were preserved, we are able to reproduce his writings here.

THE HISTORY OF MY DISEASE

by D. L. Parkinson

This is the story of my life. My biography, which is in fact the history of a wicked disease. The story of the genesis of the disease, its course, its rises and falls . . .

The story begins in Russia, in Mitrofanovsk, on the property of my father, Lavrentiy Akakyevich Parkinson. The irony of fate arranged my arrival in the world so that it was accompanied by morbid circumstances. My mother, Jevdokya Fyodorovna, following the typical cliché of Russian decadence at the time, died in childbirth. My father, who never drank before, immediately fell into inebriation. As if he had been waiting for a loved one to die so that he would have a reason to surrender to self-destruction. Not out of grief: the intentional death of women in childbirth, calculated to cause pity and respect among the neighbors, was still a common thing back then. He was drinking because of Dostoyevsky. Lavrentiy Akakyevich was hoping that Dostoyevsky, then at the peak of his fame, would notice him and dignify him with an episode in one of his novels. He knew the author of the *Karamazovs* quite well. But Dostoyevsky was not interested in polite, pale, uninteresting noblemen. He was interested in crime, filth, and vice. It was the golden age of realism. Writers drew inspiration for their work from real events. Their protagonists were men of flesh and blood. Even if there were no events worthy of artistic attention, the writers did not hesitate to make them happen. To organize intrigues that ended in murder and scandal. To create a reality which they would later develop artistically.

My father, Lavrentiy Akakyevich, decided to fight for his place in literature. The Parkinsons' dacha in Mitrofanovsk became a refuge for artists, anarchists, drunks, Fools for Christ, religious thinkers, incognito revolutionaries, and false prophets, so that Fyodor Mikhailovich would have the most ideal possible working conditions. A licentious international brotherhood that did not obey laws of any kind began to meet there, dedicated to drunkenness and orgies. From time to time, Dostoyevsky would also show up to gamble and lose enormous sums of other people's money. Despite the crazed drinking binges, Lavrentiy Akakyevich managed to preserve a certain nobility of character. His respect for the great writer gradually grew into religious fanaticism; he sold his properties for pennies, then the properties of his neighbors, and finally the properties of complete strangers, so that he could give the author of the *Karamazovs* non-returnable loans which, again, allowed Fyodor Mikhailovich to lose money unhindered and deepen his desperation, from which arose his stylistically rough pages of prose, to some people overly radiant, to others overly syrupy. In return, my father expected to be honored with a small episode in one of the writer's books. In order to occupy a humble place in those crepuscular pages where dubious creatures ramble about and it is constantly snowing, to spark the writer's inspiration, the misfortunate nobleman devoted himself to unimaginable extravagances and bizarre behaviors. He far exceeded the madness of most of Dostoyevsky's protagonists, and everyone agreed: Lavrentiy Akakyevich deserved at least fifty lines or so. But, like all big writers, Dostoyevsky was a big bastard. In a conversation with Chernyshevsky—for whom it is not certain whether he was even alive at the time—Fyodor Mikhailovich shamelessly derided his host and benefactor. Driven to the brink of desperation, my father headed off to Moscow and killed an old woman. And he almost succeeded in his undertaking: immediately after Dostoyevsky read the news about the event in *Vjedomosti,* he visited his Muse and began working on *Crime and Punishment.* But, surprise, surprise! O, the contemptibility! Instead of my father, the murderer appears in the novel to be some sort of imaginary Raskolnikov.

Did Dostoyevsky write *Demons* based on his own meager spiritual experience? That question still awaits an answer. Our dacha and the events in it far exceed the talent and ability of Dostoyevsky to recognize in them the epicenter of the Empire's disintegration, the carcinoma of the revolution whose metastasis was nearing the heart of Russia—Moscow. Dostoyevsky was a genius, I admit, but in the wrong field. He was meant to be a genius engineer, but he wanted to write even though he was unable to come up with a plot, but rather found inspiration for his clumsy novels in the crime sheets. In fact, he was not a writer but a black priest. The Faust of Russian literature. His novels contributed to the disintegration of traditional values and to creating a representation of Russians as foolish, bloodthirsty monsters incomparably greater than all the secret societies of revolutionaries who would later simply turn his poetics into politics. With Dostoyevsky, realism became more powerful than reality. The scourge of his popularity devastated Mother Russia, desecrated the Third Rome, the cradle of golden Orthodoxy. After Dostoyevsky, instead of the variety and colorfulness of the Russian soul, all that was left were five psychological types of Russians. The Stavrogin, Raskolnikov, Marmeladov, Lebeziatnikov, and Svidrigailov types.

How different was Dostoyevsky from my father, the pioneer of self-destruction, the forerunner of *body art,* one of the doyens of Russian decomposition, who was among the first to realize the saving grace of disintegration. It never occurred to Dostoyevsky to at least put Lavrentiy Akakyevich in a short story. He knew that, however small the episode, the incidental hero would cast a shadow over the author. "For Russia to be saved," my father often said, "it must first rot and ferment, it must transform itself into a new quality by means of sublimation." In those words I recognize the influence of M. I. Khalakhurov, the mesmerist and alchemist, a frequent guest in Mitrofanovsk, who set up an alchemist laboratory in the basement of the dacha, and with the assistance of Lavrentiy Akakyevich Parkinson attempted to turn copper into gold. The experiment ultimately did result in the transmutation of metal, but in the opposite direction. Instead of gold, our alchemists got a large amount of worthless tin. Khalakhurov blamed his failure on the absence of avarice in his host and helper. "Lavrentiy Akakyevich, if you want to get gold, you have to adore it, to want it passionately, because the noble skills of Alchemy do not work only through natural forces, but also through incomparably more commanding powers of the soul." My father, however, knew an easier way to get gold, and in doing so not to fall so low as to love it as well. He sold a few more neighbors' plantations (they were to be turned into *kolhozi* in a few years anyway), and he invested the rather large income in the procurement of champagne and delicacies, in generous stipends for itinerate acting companies, and in even more generous tips for dubious young beauties, living vessels for the obscure rituals of sexual magic led by the infamous Gurdjieff. The largest sums still went into the bottomless pocket of Fyodor Mikhailovich, from whence the money flowed into the pockets and purses of dodgy gamblers and casinos.

The stormy events at our dacha only seemed chaotic. That is now clear because, as recent discoveries in the field of subatomic physics have concluded, chaos rests on a foundation of strict regularities, far too complicated for our primitive understanding of order. (Ultimately, isn't all the poverty of western conceptions of regularity condensed in the scene of a firing squad that, in perfect formation, fires a volley into the heart of an innocent man.) But, at that time, chaos was still just chaos. If you bribed the local authorities in a timely and generous fashion, then chaos was not chaos. Due to the blessings of corruption, the Dionysian celebrations in Mitrofanovsk were to continue without cessation for a few more riotous years. The fame of the Parkinson's dacha unstoppably spread across the breadth of Russia and attracted more and more adherents. If we squint, we will see Rasputin in that infernal round-dance as well, stopping on the way to the Petersburg palace. Since sin attracts holiness with a magnetic power, one morning Zosima the Elder also appeared in Mitrofanovsk. "Lavrentiy Akakyevich," said the holy elder, "you have no idea how close you are to salvation. You have touched the bottom of hell. It is enough for you to honestly repent, and you will be in heaven." And the answer came, "Father Zosima, it is surely true if you say so, but I'm very tired and first I need some really good sleep." Zosima the Elder crossed himself and whispered, "This man has completely renounced himself. Lavrentiy Akakyevich is saved."

Lavrentiy Akakyevich Parkinson never neglected my education and upbringing for a moment. From my earliest childhood, my care was handled by, in the conventional sense a fictitious, but strict, French governess, Mademoiselle Delmas. My days were filled with learning foreign languages, piano lessons, the reading of classical literature, and so on. At the age of eight, I already spoke Latin better than Russian (which, among other things, I never quite mastered and which I never liked to speak.)[5] By the age of fifteen, thanks to the cosmopolitan company that gathered in the house, along with French I was also fluent in English, German, Spanish, and Turkish. I also knew the languages of the Book: ancient Greek and Hebrew. At sixteen, I was already seven feet tall, an entire eight centimeters taller than the two meters and five centimeters of my height after the move to the metric system and some miscalculations. With my father's blessing—at the time he was unable to give me anything else, Dostoyevsky had squandered it all—I departed for Yasnaya Polyana, to pay homage to my idol Lev Tolstoy. (What is it about us Parkinsons that drives us to grovel before writers?). Old man Lev received me. To my great disappointment, the old man, reeking of garlic, belching, and casting lascivious looks at a maid, did not fit into the image of the Golden Calf with a long beard and *rubashka* who had written *War and Peace*, whom in my naiveté I had placed in the center of my pantheon. Later, I was to describe my disappointment to my namesake, the poet Demyan Bedny: "There's not much to say. The only difference between Dostoyevsky and Tolstoy is that Tolstoy doesn't gamble." It can only be conjectured as to whether the abyss with Tolstoy on one side and his work on the other, endlessly far away from each other, had a crucial influence on me, made me despise literature, art in general, and dedicate myself to spiritual pathology. Whatever the case, the early years of the twentieth

5. I'm convinced that the wearisome history of the Russian nation owes a lot to the orthography of the Russian language, especially the softening sign (Ъ) and the hard "i" (Ы). The first softens the language too much, and the second actually makes it too harsh. Nations are just a bodily expression of the language they speak. In the case of Russia, either too complacent or too cruel.

century saw me obsessed with natural sciences. If the proverbial impracticality of the Parkinsons for secular business had not gotten involved, the world would have learned of entropy much earlier. "Every effort made to introduce order into a system results in the increase in disorder," I wrote in a letter to Vladimir Solovyov. The topic of the letter, however, was not theoretical physics, which one could conclude from a cursory glance, but a much more subtle theological question about the ratio between personal effort and God's mercy on the road to a man's salvation. Solovyov maintained that personal effort was crucial, that the doctrine of mercy was the direct product of endemic Russian laziness and disorder. I, on the other hand, believed that Mercy (grace) was the only power able to transform human nature's depravity. In our ongoing correspondence which lasted several years (and even continued for a time after Solovyov's death), I composed the contours of a theory stating that esthetic efforts, in fact, lead to a reduction of the internal chaos of ascetics, but in return increase the mayhem of those people near them. I supported this theory with practically undeniable evidence. "The more monasteries and monks in a country, the more disorder there is. Is there a better example than Russia? On the other hand, the most well-ordered and disciplined countries, like Holland, Germany, and England, have no monasteries or monks. The wish for a man to be saved is an expression of the greatest arrogance. No one *deserves* it." Solovyov, however, was relentless. "Well, what then, Demyan Lavrentyevich?" the religious thinker was dismissive. "At least several thousand people will be saved in Russia, but no one in the countries you mention. There are fake states of chaos which owe their 'chaoticness' to the chaoticness of our perception. Just as there also exist fake 'harmonies' and illusions of order, behind which are concealed unimaginable instabilities. Both of these states, however, are interwoven in a fantastic multitude of intermediate forms. What it comes down to is this: how can we utilize chaos instead of wasting our energy on attempts to defeat it (which is impossible) or avoid it (which is even less possible)."

This, in fact, is not the story of my life. That story cannot be written. For the simple reason that I have often changed my identity. Although, unfortunately, not often enough. It is dangerous to have only one identity. Over time, you grow accustomed to your name, habits, virtues and vices, and suddenly you get comfortable within yourself. In the morass. A man begins to love himself, which is the same as spiritual death. And not just spiritual. Because quickly the fear arises that *that* will die one day. A man equates himself with his own identity, with that phantom, to such an extent that he completely forgets about his real *self*, and is no longer able to realize that this false identity is in fact the very fear of death. The secret was revealed to me by Zosima the Elder during his frequent visits to our vice-ridden dacha. Although, the truth is (now I can say it because they are both dead) that was not Zosima the Elder, but Isaiah the Elder disguised as Zosima the Elder. Just as Zosima was also disguised as Isaiah. I would not reject the possibility that both "Zosima" and "Isaiah" were actually masks of identity, and that only the two of them knew who they were. Because you can only be a true mystic if nobody knows you exist. (In the true Orthodox tradition, it is a mortal sin to be anyone.) If even the two of them, experienced ascetics, holy men, thought it prudent to conceal who they were, imagine the amount of danger we mere sinners are exposed to. "My son," Zosima said to me, "your name, posture, habits, memories, all of those are a wide-open door for the devil. You shouldn't dare be the same person for more than a year, two at most. You must especially never become well-known. Because it's possible to renounce a false identity, but fame can be renounced by no one, without the help of God. Take your father as an example. Even though he drinks, and even though, as much as possible in his advanced age, he engages in debauchery, blasphemy, and all sorts of misdeeds, he will be saved because he really doesn't care who he is, and most of the time doesn't even know. If it weren't for his vain desire for Fyodor Mikhailovich to mention him in a story, he would be a real holy man."

I'm not the best pupil of Zosima the Elder. I'm also not among the worst. Somehow, it was discovered that I existed, but no one was able to say with certainty who I was. My contemporaries interpreted that as vanity, insecurity, as the fear of appearing to be from somewhere. In actuality, it was the fear of false identity, which I overcame by relying on more and more fake identities, such fantastic ones that the danger was minimal that I might end up believing in any of them. Relieved of the worry about "the self," because those "selves" were disposable, ephemeral, exchangeable at any time for some other, I could dedicate myself to my disease, to patient work on researching, perfecting, and popularizing it.

My disease could have saved the world. If only I had managed to infect it. Here and there, true, I succeeded with great effort to infect several hospitals and cities, along with a few inspired people who would use the disease, masked in a political program, for the benefit of their nations. Turkey, for example, would look completely different if Kemal Paşa did not sufficiently despise the profanity of health and instead sufficiently worshipped pathology. But, overall, I was defeated. The reckless and superficial ideology of health repressed my illness and condemned the world to an untimely death. Moreover, it erased all mention of Parkinson's disease. (It was spoken of only in works of fiction.) To make the deception complete, it was later ascribed to a certain Dr. Parkinson, an insignificant provincial doctor; it was a set of symptoms of which trembling was the most characteristic, symptoms which altogether are not even a disease in the classical sense, but just what is called *weakness* in the Orthodox tradition. Or, something more modern: fatigue induced by overindulgence.

Every drunk and every sinner have Parkinson's disease in that form. I'm not exaggerating when I say that all of humankind suffers from such a low-ranked illness. Its primitiveness, the lack of enlightenment and refinement, make people experience it as health.

The real Parkinson's disease basically has no symptoms whatsoever. No lowly trembling. No fatigue, unconsciousness, erratic pulse, high blood pressure and temperature, poor blood count, and other piffle that arise from the panicky pursuit of health. None of those things. And yet, even though sufferers feel great, it is the most horrible of all diseases. The mother of all diseases which gives birth to the rest of illnesses, even though, I say, it has no symptoms whatsoever. I discovered it early on. While still in my childhood. In the morning, after waking up, I had the habit (and who doesn't) of lying in bed in a state of temporary bliss, watching the deceptive play of sunbeams on the walls of my room. Until one morning that bliss was harshly interrupted by a question which *arose by itself*: How does anything exist at all? The gaping abyss of nothingness appeared before my naïve internal eyes. I instantly realized the horrible truth: existence is a disease. An ugly growth on the being. Whatever that being might be.

Immediately I prayed to God and repressed that tortuous experience. The illness was still in its early phase, and the Lord, thanks to the flood of sin in my father's dacha, poured a flood of mercy on those who turned to him from that place of black magic and debauchery. But I never forgot that fateful morning. Health causes forgetfulness, but I had encountered the disease. Though at the time, or for many years later, I didn't realize that it is in fact the cure.

The world lies submerged in chaos. Things are not in their right places. Those which should be joined are separated; those which should be separated are joined. Things are incomparably worse in the unexplored fields of psychology. Disarray really rules there. Not to mention the so-called "exact" sciences. *Good* and *evil* have long since been replaced with the relative concepts of *pleasant* and *unpleasant*. Man's primary duty: to suffer and to endure pain, which has perfidiously been proclaimed to be a disease, a pathological state. Especially in the deceitful spirit of the epoch called masochism, named after a certain German baron who was prepared for anything except suffering. To the extent that even those brave husbands who would gladly suffer and endure pain are forced to express gentleness so that they are not proclaimed to be perverts.

Then one day a few years later, the disease suddenly manifested itself with all its might. I was headed to Demidovo, some fifteen versts from Mitrofanovsk to pick up some money from somebody-or-other to whom my father had sold who-knows-whose land, when somewhere about halfway, I had a powerful fainting spell and fell into the dust. I thought I was dying. My limbs were shaking and jerking uncontrollably; I was trembling; my organs ceased working one by one. My heart stopped beating for several minutes (or at least it seemed to have), my lungs were completely paralyzed. Every cell in my organism, and there are plenty of them, hurt individually . . . If absolute suffering exists, I experienced it that day. This was a good lesson for a young man who was slowly sliding into the heresy of Darwinism and becoming a fan of the obscure cult of the spontaneous creation of life from the primordial soup. There, on the dusty country road, God brutally revealed, no matter how healthy in the medical sense, what biological life is when the beneficial energies supporting it are withdrawn. Believe me, no one would wish to live.

However, the basic characteristic of the real Parkinson's disease is that the person gets healthier and more resistant after every attack (each of which is worse than the one before). As long as he doesn't seek medical help. Doctors ruin everything. But more about that later. On returning to Mitrofanovsk, my pockets stuffed with rubles, I stopped off at a tavern, ordered vodka and pickles, asked the owner for a pen and paper, and sat in the corner to write down my first reactions, in the light of a tallow-candle. It went something like this: life in itself is a disease. For the simple reason that, as Genesis tells us, this is not real life but just making ends meet, incompletion. In such a "life," the sickest are those who are seemingly the healthiest, who feel good living it. In the light of those revelations in the tavern, I realized that health is a subtle form of insensibility, and if you like, a lack of soul. Mindless striving for health, I wrote on, produces an entire series of vices. I cast a glance around. Small groups of drunks, thieves, prostitutes, and bums in the tavern. And I thought: if only they were besieged by a disease, if they got an ulcerous lump, if they were struck by tuberculosis, they surely wouldn't be here, engaged in hideous vices, but they would be lying in bed and, since they don't have money for a doctor, praying to God for help. That's the way it is, as the timeworn proverb says: a sick man thinks of only one thing—getting well. A "healthy" man, to the contrary, has lots of intentions, wishes, and plans on his mind, which inevitably drive him to illness.

Many things were revealed to me in that country tavern packed with the demimonde; there is no university library in which those things could be learned. Let's take the mystique of disease in the

New Testament. Jesus, in fact, does not interact with the healthy and hearty. (The healthy were to crucify him in the end.) His powers are demonstrated on the cripples, the lame, the blind, the leprous, the barren women . . . Is it possible, I wondered, that not a single theologian or philosopher has understood that illness is actually the gateway through which divine energy enters, and that the sufferings we ascribe to disease are in fact the birth pangs in which the new man is born, as described by St. Paul? How is it possible, I thought, that none of the myriad theologians, doctors (except maybe Paracelsus) ever noticed that one shouldn't treat illness, but rather deliver the patient from health . . .

As always, after ecstasy came the fall. Excited by the profound insight into the mystique of pathology, well-steeped in vodka, I thought I was healthy again. Typical beginner's mistake. A man should never think that he is above his disease. But I, may God forgive me, believed that I would reveal the truth to the world and stand shoulder to shoulder with the prophets. Pure stupidity. The days of the prophets are gone forever. Now are the days of politics.

Parkinsonism was not supposed to be a religious doctrine, nor even a branch of medicine, but rather a political movement.

But I, that evening, couldn't have known it . . .

To be continued.

INCUBATION

> "My heart panteth, my strength faileth me: as for the
> light of mine eyes,
> it also is gone from me. My lovers and my friends stand
> aloof from my sores,
> and my kinsmen stand afar off."
>
> Psalms 38:12

1905. Demyan Lavrentyevich met Joseph Vissarionovich Jughashvili and initiated him into the secrets of Parkinson's disease. Jughashvili joined the revolutionary movement.

In an obscure Moscow journal, *Afterlife,* a supposed answer from F. M. Dostoyevsky appeared to Parkinson's text *The History of My Disease*:

A RESPONSE TO A PASQUINADE
by F. M. Dostoyevsky

Although I died in 1882, instead of 1881 as it is usually stated, I did not live a second longer than I did. The misunderstanding arose because of those fatal thirteen days of difference between the Gregorian calendar and the Julian which was used in Russia at the time. It does not matter. Dead writers should not appear in public. They should not do so even when alive. But there are some things that I just cannot get past without comment. Like getting past the toxic little brochures, for example, in which Demyan Lavrentyevich Parkinson spews out a bunch of filthy lies. Yes, I was a gambler, I do not deny it. But it is the fruit of a sick mind to claim that I financially wrecked his father, that I forced him into Siberian exile, and that Lavrentiy Parkinson sold others' property because of my debts. Like the lie that I was an advocate of the replacement of the Julian calendar with the Gregorian. Or, most nonsensical of all, that my novels cleared the way to the October Revolution.

The truth is quite different.

There was no more vociferous opponent to the transition to the Gregorian calendar than me. Back when the "free thinkers,"—slaves to the most horrible errors—were demanding, for the sake of modernization, that the Empire's calendar be harmonized with the European, I openly supported the Church in its resistance to that frivolous toying with time, that hellish rush to step into the future ahead of time. Just as the geomorphology and climate of certain countries differ, their time also differs. The time of Russia is not the same time as that of Germany. For ages, the thirteen-day difference between European time and Russian time prevented the influx of negative influences: atheism, money-grubbing, enterprise, fashion, and especially the root of all evil—avarice—which I fought against by gambling away all my earnings down to the last ruble. And I was right for supporting the Church despite the smirks of the socialists. It is true that Russia will adopt the Gregorian calendar only after the revolution. But that only proves my point. Because fatuous changes in the measurement of time do not produce consequences in the future, but in the past. Even a few Protestants are aware of this. Why, the philosopher-atheist Nietzsche moved about in a period of his life by taking four steps forward, then three backward; then again, four forward, three backward, just to neutralize the unnatural acceleration of central European time, and it made his thinking processes radiate. But in doing so, he incurred hatred and damnation. He was to die, as it proved, in complete disarray, from a disease unknown to medicine, perhaps the very same one suffered by the sycophant Parkinson.

The Parkinsons are not even Russians. Although they are some sort of nobility, their lineage does not reach further back than Samuil Longfelovich Parkinson, a Scot, or maybe an Irishman, an army medic captured on one of the battlefields and brought to Saint Petersburg, where he became famous for his salves to treat venereal diseases. It is said that he personally healed Kneeb Piter Komandor of gonorrhea, who, as a gesture of gratitude, rewarded him with a sack of gold, property in a distant *guberniya*, and a nobleman's title. All the later Parkinsons were doctors, up until the incompetent Lavrentiy Akakyevich, a fantasizer and dreamer, who was essentially nothing. And his son, Demyan, took a step further from the guild of doctors and took refuge in the guild of valetudinarians. However, if one dug deeper into the past of his forebears, it would not surprise me if it turned out that the roots of the Parkinson genealogical tree were found deep in the fertile ground of my imagination. In the pre-epileptic visions I was prone to in moments of penury. In my notes and sketches for fantastic unwritten novels. It wouldn't be the first time for a visionary to disappear, vanish, and for his visions to solidify and emerge on the surface of the empirical. Whatever the case, it is true that I visited their dacha. Many people passed by there. But that I borrowed money from Lavrentiy Akakyevich—that is not true. Except maybe a few rubles a couple of times. Perhaps I would have borrowed more, but Parkinson was an absolute pauper. The obscure alchemist Khalakhurov convinced gullible Lavrentiy Akakyevich to increase the little remaining family gold through an alchemical experiment. They did something wrong, instead turning the gold into tin. Generally speaking, everything Parkinson did can be described in a symbolic sense as the transmutation of gold into tin. It is not to go without mention that the medical skills of the Parkinsons were based on personal experience, on the syphilis of Samuel Longfelovich which, in ever worsening form, was passed from generation to generation, to the point that the disease reached its peak in the person of Demyan Lavrentyevich, in some ways the very *incarnation* of syphilis, where we are no longer dealing with a man carrying a disease, but with a disease that had become a man.

I am by nature sympathetic to the sick, the poor, and the humiliated. In the Orthodox tradition, illness is valued as an important stage on the path to salvation. So where did my contempt for Demyan Lavrentyevich, the sickest of all the people I ever met, come from? Perhaps because instead of contrition and repentance, illness aroused pride and self-confidence in him. So that he did not even think of being cured, but, if possible, of infecting others.

My epilepsy, after all, owes a lot to Demyan Parkinson. Before I started visiting the damn dacha, a story I probably conceived myself, the attacks were very rare. Earlier, it was mild fainting, temporary loss of balance, quite tolerable nausea, and dizziness. But then things got worse. The naïve will say that, over time, disease worsens by the nature of things, but although I have no evidence, I would rather attribute the worsening to the magical intervention of Demyan Lavrentyevich. Take the example of his parents. His mother died in childbirth. From sepsis, they said. However, I am more inclined to suspect that this was a murder. For him, the late Yevdokia Fyodorovna was just a kind of incubator, a larva, the logistics for intrauterine survival, which he rejected as superfluous the moment he was born. Father Lavrentiy, a man who had never drunk a drop of alcohol before, started drinking like a fish less than an hour after his birth.

Something's rotten in Denmark.

Demyan, however, attributes the cause of his father's suicidal intoxication to my malice; my refusal to dedicate a few lines in prose to Lavrentiy Akakyevich. Which is true. But I have never dedicated a single word to anyone. For purely practical reasons. If I had indulged the ambitions of acquaintances, my collected works would have been an ordinary census, a kind of Moscow and St. Petersburg telephone directory before the existence of the telephone. There is more. In realistic novels, the characters must be fictional. That's why I came up with the most incredible surnames in order to avoid the possibility that a protagonist might have a double beyond the covers of the book. In vain! It turned out that all these surnames exist neatly recorded in the registry books. Yes, every last one. Including two Marmeladovs and even three Smerdyakovs. That is not the end to Demyan's insinuations. Rumor has it that Lavrentiy Akakyevich, in a desperate desire to impose himself on me as a literary character, went to Moscow and killed an old woman, and that I, having read the news in the newspaper, immediately sat down to write *Crime and Punishment*. He says sarcastically, "He had a visit from his muse." Is there an end to these insults?

I don't know if Lavrentiy Akakyevich really killed an old woman. I doubt that even he knows. It is possible. People steeped in vodka with a high percentage of methyl alcohol have done worse things. And even if he did, that proves nothing. Not a day passes without some old woman getting killed. But for the purposes of *Crime and Punishment*, I myself, in the literary sense of course, killed my grandmother. For the sake of the plot. Because any careful reader knows that I'm not interested in crime, but in punishment. The agony of a bad conscience. The facilitation of repentance. The willingness to forbear. It is a completely different matter that, after reading the novel, a student who, by chance, really identified with Raskolnikov, actually killed an old woman, and the case was later published in the press. That was something different, however. That is the influence of literature on reality. Just how many young men killed themselves after Goethe's *Werther*. In the ambivalent relationship between literature and reality, the influences do not flow, as the superficial realists believe, in the direction of reality-literature, but, on the contrary, literature-reality. Mother Russia will soon be convinced of this when the *Manifesto of the Communist Party* becomes the social order. Is that a reason to give up on literature and sink into the depths of barbarism? Not at all. There are no coincidences. The law of probability, which is increasingly displacing Imperial and Divine laws, is the most common balderdash. It states: the probability of someone being killed by lightning is a paltry 0.00007 percent. But I say: that there are people who will die from lightning has a probability of 100%. There is no other way for them to leave this world. Everything that happens to us is completely determined and certain. Our feeling of uncertainty stems from our unwillingness to carry our cross, to live our lives constantly trying to be someone else.

Here, confused young Parkinson is partially right. Even liars of his type occasionally write something true. Although in such situations, I advise extreme caution. It cannot be otherwise with a man who claims to be two meters and five centimeters tall, although he was not, if I remember correctly, taller than a meter and a half. Ascribing it to the inaccuracy of calculating units of measurement when replacing our old measures with the metric system does not help.

It is just another innovation, which, together with the removal of some of our letters (they say superfluous, and I say that there are too few of them in every alphabet) and the transition to the Gregorian calendar, is turning Russia into a colony of the Vatican. Let us leave aside for a moment the spiritual dimension of the problem and turn to the ever more visible empiricism. Due to the sloppy conversion of the state's territory from square versts to square kilometers, as usual to our detriment, Russia lost 125,000 square kilometers of the most fertile land, which, also thanks to dubious calculations, now belongs to Mongolia and China.

For now, I have nothing more to say. I'm not even sure that I even said this. Nothing is certain any longer. I'll shut up. I'll go for a walk through some of my descriptions of Moscow's streets, where dubious characters roam about and where November snow flurries always fall.

In order to avoid the attention of Imperial Censorship, Demyan Lavrentyevich resorted to cunning. He broke the *Tractatus antiheliocentricus* into smaller units and at the end of 1903 published its first four pages.

TRACTATUS ANTIHELIOCENTRICUS

PART ONE

Politics has imperceptibly carried out a coup. In Greek, politics means the same as urbanism in Neo-Latin: organizing, supplying, and fortifying the city. Basically, it is a series of routine tasks whose goal is the smooth functioning of city roads and fortifications. But as chronology (extremely unreliable, as we shall see) approaches the modern age, we notice that politics is going far beyond the domain of urbanism, encompassing and absorbing an ever-widening circle of things, so at this moment there is nothing that is not a political problem. It is as if the infamous separation of church and state was not performed—as it was announced—in order to free earthly affairs from the influence of the otherworld, but in order to raise worldly affairs to the otherworld and become a metaphysical entity which, instead of serving man, begins to rule his life.

***

This text seeks to illuminate the processes of the politicization of things that by their nature cannot be the object of political decision-making; it strives to point out that, in the background of the generally accepted political mythology of the modern age, there is no concern for progress but an aspiration for the restoration of pagan cults and the nomadic way of life, which have now been transformed into cults of the machine, science, progress, democracy, etc.

***

To talk about politics means to talk about the city, about the history of the city and its rise, and about the causes of its decline. There are several schools of thought as to why the city came about. One emphasizes trade as the origin of the city, the other considers it to be war. Both cover part of the truth, but neither provides an answer to the question: why did a certain number of people give up the nomadic life and build the first permanent settlement? In considering the origin of the city, the spiritual dimension of urbanism is mostly neglected. The share of trade and war in the development of the idea of the city is indisputable, but the decision to move to a sedentary life must have been preceded by a spiritual insight into the hopelessness found in the chaotic freedom of movement. The spiritual principle of the city is evidenced by the later developed symbolic and mystical dimension of urbanism, guarded for centuries by the secret fraternities of builders. Modern Freemasonry is—quite in line with the low levels to which the modern city has fallen—only a distorted and profane relic.

***

The nomadic way of life only seems like a realm of non-constraint and freedom. The tribes that roam the steppes are subjected to necessity and forced to follow the determined rhythms of the elements. Such tribes are, like the monsoons or the change of seasons, more natural phenomena than human communities are.

***

In order for people to gather in a religious community, they first had to stop and build a city and thus symbolically and physically separate themselves from the natural elements by the first state institution: the city walls. The state at that time was religious because it assumed that the connection between people could be made exclusively through a connection with the divine. Basically, the state (and politics in general) is a fortified and organized city, the materialized idea of the center, around which order then spreads to the surrounding areas in concentric circles. At first, only the center—the city—was clearly defined, the external borders were diffuse. In the modern state, however, only the external borders, i.e., the periphery, are precisely determined, while the center is diffuse and, often in recent history, defined and located in random places. It has been completely forgotten that the key thing for urbanism is to determine the place where the city will be built. The location of the city decisively influences its development, its destiny, as well as the destiny of the state that emerges in its surroundings.

For a long time now, however, urban planning has considered exclusively economic and transportation aspects, completely ignoring geophysical, climatic, geological, historical, and all other aspects affecting the fate of the city. The ancient Chinese architects, from whom the West always learns too little, aspired, for example, to situate the capital city in the geographical center of the empire. The center of the capital was reserved for the Forbidden City, in which, again, the Imperial Palace was located in the center, designed to represent a miniature copy of the empire. We can ask ourselves to what extent the somewhat lethargic but undeniable stability of China depends on the attention given to the abovementioned symbolic architectural and urban materialization of the idea of harmony, which was abandoned in the West, where things went to the opposite extreme: abstract geometrization.

***

The very meaning of the city walls, considered mainly from a defensive aspect, is incomparably more complex. It can be said that their defensive role is secondary compared to their symbolism. First and foremost: the walls define the urban space, determine the center and the original orientation on the compass. Furthermore, the walls separate the cultivated space of the city from the elemental space of nature. Preventing the penetration of external elements inwards, the city walls simultaneously stop the negative processes that flow from the city outwards. Pollution began with the removal of city walls and in a sense, it is nothing but the metastasis of the city that has gone beyond its natural boundaries. Many pages inspired by the Enlightenment are devoted to lamentations over the hygienic conditions prevailing in the traditional city; even more were written in honor of modern, highly dubious hygiene, ignoring the fact that the apparent and temporary removal of waste from the city necessarily leads to irreversible environmental pollution, pollution that already indicates the proximity of epidemics and diseases, previously unknown in the world.

***

It is no exaggeration to say that the downfall of Western civilization begins with the removal of city walls—walls perceived as an obstacle to the oncoming expansion of the state, which is expanding outward from the city center, attempting to establish control over entire territories. It is the beginning of the politicization of space and the later meddling of politics in the domains of science, ethics, aesthetics, and even cosmology.

***

The beginning of all the great troubles, the mother of all later revolutions, is the replacement of the geocentric view of the world with the heliocentric one. The doctrine of heliocentrism was really a revolution in politics, not in science. The displacement of the Earth from the center of the universe was not aimed at bringing order to celestial mechanics; it was indeed the apotheosis of arbitrariness and disorder. In the Christian tradition, the Earth's central position has nothing to do with the relations between celestial bodies and their arrangement in space; it is the center in an inner, spiritual sense, placing Adam as the central point of Creation.

***

Once accepted as a scientific fact, the theory that the Earth is one of the countless celestial bodies on the galactic periphery slowly destroyed the strongholds of human spirituality and true dignity, in parallel with the humanistic ideologized apotheosis of humanity. The cosmological provincialization of the Earth fed the rise of provincialism, particularization, and desacralization, while creating terrible alienation in the human community.

***

Space suddenly gained importance, regardless of whether it is infertile, unnecessary, or an inaccessible part of a territory. A kind of sacralization of the soil, previously limited to cult sites and burial grounds, now raises "every foot" of state territory to the status of "sanctuary," jealously defending itself from the footsteps of foreigners. The cult of the soil which, together with the simultaneously growing cult of blood, would show the full force of its sinister nature only in this century, introducing tribal, nomadic models of life into Christian civilization, and laying the foundation for a new idolatry.

***

The mania of controlling the territory, which, to be fair, realistically needs to be guarded from the aspirations of the surrounding states, led to the growing control of the state government over its subjects, which was never to be halted again. The city became only one part of the state's territory. The city wall—as the boundary between the city and its surroundings—disappeared, the city lost its identity, and all the negative influences, both from the outside inwards and those from the inside out, flowed freely in both directions, undermining traditional institutions. The city spread uncontrollably into the environs, polluting them, and pagan rituals from the surroundings entered the city unhindered, eroding its very foundations.

Despite the fragmentary nature of the publication, Imperial Censorship banned the brochure.

1904. Demyan Lavrentyevich performed an open-heart operation in Tbilisi, the first in the history of surgery.

The mystical triangle, the symbol of parkinsonism, designed by the then little-known Malevich, came into use.

The story *The Final Days and Death of Jakob Böhme,* published under the pseudonym J. Schwenekpfeld, was published in Paris. Although written in a boring, strained style, reading the story is less tedious than reading the ten-year chronology of events that preceded the fateful year of 1914. Time will show that the writing is actually a visionary description of the last days and death of Parkinson himself.

The Final Days and Death of Jakob Böhme

by J. Schwenekpfeld

1

Towards the end of his life, Jakob Böhme ate nothing but his manuscripts. His meager meals consisted of two sheets of paper, square, elegantly written in minuscule. After the meal, he would drink a glass of water and that was it. We three apprentices, Caspar, Otto, and I, Schwenekpfeld, were very worried about this: we were worried about the master's health, and then about the damage that this unusual diet threatened to inflict on future generations, depriving them of his writings. However, he cared little for his health, even less for the future and our cajoling to stop his cruel fasting. Patiently, with his characteristic cheerfulness and perseverance, he waited for the spiritual knowledge to be born in us that all worry is ungodly and sinful, that people gladly indulge in that seemingly unpleasant feeling in order to satisfy their own vanity and gloat about their non-existent goodness. However, when we informed him of our decision to make copies of all his works, he did not object, primarily because we were illiterate. And on the condition that our daily work of tanning, drying, and tailoring hides did not suffer at all because of it. "My children," he said, "it is a greater work to put shoes on a peasant than to copy a hundred books. In a mystical way, you are also putting on those shoes and heading toward salvation along the safe and narrow way of humility; for '*of making many books there is no end, and all is vanity.'"* He may not have believed in the success of our endeavor—I have already said that we were illiterate—but he believed in our faith in the impossible; in our faith he saw the first step of spiritual ascension; he even encouraged us, knowing that we would have to work hard at night, malnourished, at the expense of sleep and rest; he rejoiced at the exhaustion, and perhaps at the diseases that would inevitably follow. He might even have hoped that, if not all, at least one of the three of us would die—a better outcome for shoemaking apprentices at the time—before fate led us to marry, have children, and suffer all the torments that come from Adam's curse. But we, being sturdy lads, had a chance to survive; Master Böhme, on the other hand, weak in his youth, had turned into his own shadow. Half a riding boot could fit in the recess in his chest. Still, without conceding to anything, he worked with us from dawn till dusk, and did not even think of obeying our persuasions and eating a bowl of hot stew from time to time.

"The devil himself speaks out from you!" he growled. "How many times have I told you what Master Valentin Weigel told me last year at the Alt Seidenberg fair: *Böhme, whatever a man takes from outside himself, from the elements and stars, be it food or drink, it is the same as the man himself. And so, if a man eats bread and drinks water or wine from the macrocosm, he is in fact consuming himself.* But I say unto you even more: as much as you take from outside, that much, and maybe more, will you have to return there. And the less you partake of the outside world, the less you owe it and the more easily it shall release you from its clutches when the time comes for you to return into yourself, where the *other world* is."

Hearing those words, all three of us were ashamed.

We realized that he really hadn't repeated Master Weigel's words that many times, because he thought we were stupid and couldn't understand their meaning. He wanted more from us, but out of gentleness and respect for our freedom, he did not want to impose anything on us. His wish was for us to understand the most urgent things from Weigel's teaching, and for each of us to compose his own "rosary." Nowadays, when piety is declining and when even the most honorable people are satisfied with simply going to church in the morning and evening, rarely, if at all, thinking of God between worship services, when no one knows what a rosary is anymore, I'll have to explain how it was in the time when I was Master Böhme's apprentice.

At that time, in order to avoid vain and devilish thoughts, every pious man repeated a short prayer aloud all day long, except when urgent business, decency, or conversation with other people prevented him from doing so. The old days! No one hid his sins; that's probably why there were fewer of them. The shame of public admission contributed to sins being easier to overcome and easier to avoid repeating them. Even the Jews had their own Jewish rosaries, only they pronounced them silently within themselves because they were composed in the Tatar language, and the superstitious suspected that they were spells, although they were not, since our Jews are hardworking and pious people. The town of Görlitz was filled with a pious bustle that created a special warmth and filled it with a feeling of intimacy and trust. Everyone knew what the other was thinking. For example, our next-door neighbor, Reinhard, the coppersmith, kept shouting all day, shouting to overcome the pounding of the hammer: "O father, Johann, it's good that you died because at least you stopped sinning, and now you can't force me to go on committing your sins in my own way." Our other neighbor, Immanuel, the potter, tried to be louder than Reinhard, exclaiming, "Just as I make this pot of clay, so the Lord made me. But this blessed pot will return to clay, and I, Immanuel, will go straight to hell if I don't fix myself, of which I have doubts." And in general, every craftsman had his own rosary, as did every merchant, and even the noblemen, I think, had their own prayers, but I cannot guarantee it because they did not mingle with us. Only Master Böhme did not have his own prayer. When Caspar once asked him how it was that he, a pious man and philosopher, did not have a rosary, he laughed and said, "I am a mystic." At the time, there were no German dictionaries, let alone words in them, especially not these sorts of words, so Otto dared to ask him for an explanation.

"I'd love to," he said. "A mystic is a man who conceals his real life. First within himself. Then he lets God worry about the rest. After that, he dedicates himself to a singular goal: to weave a web around his personality that will lead everyone's attention, including his closest relatives, down the wrong path. He must, like an actor in a circus, construct a completely improbable and different character, act as a bully, a pervert, a madman, because if only someone really knew what was happening to his soul, he would immediately know it, and his work and effort could easily go to ruin. So, the entire enterprise of a mystic is to spin lies and spread them around, but he must do it so convincingly that there is no difference between, say, a brute pretending to be a brute and a brute who really is one. Just as I am a highly esteemed shoemaker whose boots are known even in Saxony, although I have nothing to do with shoemaking and I have to make great efforts every day to bring my deception to perfection and so make it the truth, because God, who in the meantime shapes the soul, does not forgive the lie by which the truth protects itself from the world. Remember this well: Cursed is he who does the opposite. Not caring at all what is going on inside him, he tries to seem pious at all times. Gentle and sublime words come out of his mouth; he behaves humbly, with dignity. He never lies. Or thinks he never lies. He gives alms. In the end, he achieves the same thing as the mystic: his deception is perfect, it is truthful, but the mystic is saved, and he is damned. Because Heaven cannot be bought."

I am writing this passage of the chronicle about the last days and the death of a great man with invisible ink, which, if you believe the alchemist Johann Trebesch, who sold it to me for a lot of money, will only become legible in 250 years. Long enough to postpone my meanness to a time when it will no longer be a scandal. Because, despite my loyalty and immeasurable love for Master Böhme, I can't remain silent about what I'm going to write now. Partly because I think it's instructive, partly because I'm a scoundrel who can't refrain from gossiping. Namely, it is difficult to understand (and even harder to write about it) the whim of the destiny that connected that sublime husband with his wife, our landlady, Katarina Kunzmann, who is doubtlessly a witch. There she is in Görlitz, still alive, although she is seven years older than Böhme, and thirty-six years have passed since his death in 1625 (not 1624, as people think) at the age of fifty. What is still said in Görlitz today is true, that Böhme received money from Katarina's father, the butcher Heinrich Kunzmann, to buy a house and open a shoemaker's shop, but as God himself is a witness, and we three apprentices can testify, Jakob Böhme married out of the purest and most edified love, which lasted until the last moment of his pristine life. Despite her unbearable temper and the hard-to-imagine humiliations to which that evil woman, Lilith's bastard child, constantly subjected him. Master Böhme was not a man who hid his shame. On the contrary! In the name of the salvation of the soul, because of which he wished that we apprentices would get sick and suffer, he enthusiastically accepted every humiliation that was to befall him. He even felt guilty or conscience-stricken if he accidentally felt a hint of bitterness while enduring Katarina's insults or fulfilling her insane wishes. "Ah, children," he once complained, "last night Katarina woke me up before dawn and ordered me to go to the forest and pick fragrant hellebore. What should I do, you know what she's like, I got up and went, but there's no hellebore. It's still too early for hellebore. When I came home empty-handed, she threw me out of the house, and I slept in the pigsty. I'm so sorry I couldn't fulfill her wish. Tonight, when we close up shop, I will definitely go to the forest again and look for hellebore." He paused, thought, and added, "And you know: pigs are wonderful creatures!" Then, quietly murmuring the Psalms of David, he continued to stitch a sole on a boot; shrouded in a haze of mixed fumes of dung and pigswill, we apprentices cried "amen" from time to time and all our work was light in that intimate atmosphere of mutual love and forgiveness.

The next day, Master Böhme suddenly ordered us to stop working; this was not his custom. Until then, he had given us all our lessons while we toiled. We sensed that something unusual was at hand. He served us each a glass of blueberry schnapps, sat on a three-legged stool and, knowing that because of his love for him we were starting to hate Katarina, he started talking to us. I am writing this upcoming part in plain ink to save the invisible stuff, and to make his sublime thoughts available for anyone to whom this history falls into their hands.

"My sons, on Sundays when you stand at Mass, you hear the priest speak of Adam and his miserable fall; and no matter how pious and honest the pastor is, and worthy of all praise, I guarantee you that he imagines Adam as, in truth a handsome, but ordinary man, as he is, as am I, and as are you. And, God forgive me, our pastor imagines heaven as the cathedral in Görlitz, only in his imagination it is overgrown with vegetation and bathed in light stronger than a thousand burning candles. Furthermore, he thinks that the Lord is watching Adam from the pulpit, from some exalted place in Eden, and giving him orders from on high. And here our pastor is right. Because for most of those who come to church, God must be like that. He, may I be forgiven for the word 'must,' he must present himself that way, because if he showed himself at least a little bit as he is, no one would believe in him. Everyone would be horrified, hide their faces, and flee as far away as possible. My children, don't think that God is terrible, far from it. God is, as far as we can know about him, just a looking glass. When we 'see' God, since God cannot be seen, we are actually seeing ourselves. Hence the fear, horror, and confusion that overwhelms us. Because God reveals in us what he otherwise hides from us out of philanthropy. *God just shows us what we are like.* That is why it is good that God does not appear, that 'no sign is given to this generation,' because otherwise people would sink into despair. Because if we really knew what we are like, we would become a hundred times worse.

"Furthermore, when the pastor says, '*male and female He created them*,' neither he nor anyone else pays attention to it. And here for the wise lies the key that unlocks many secrets. Pay attention, my sons! In one, thus, in the beginning there were two. In His wisdom, the Lord chose to spare us all that we are now suffering. He wanted everything to go smoothly, for everything to go 'from light into light.' And if only Adam, our primordial father, had not made a mistake, everything would be the same as it is now. I would be Böhme, you would be Caspar, you Otto, you Schwenekpfeld; and everything that exists would exist, and everything that needs to happen would come into being naturally and peacefully, without turbulence, troubles, and wars, if only Adam had not erred in his ways.

The coppersmith Reinhard has no idea how right he is when he curses his father all day. We should all be crying out all day, 'Father Adam, it is good that you died, for if you had not, our evil would be eternal.' My children, I can see that you're astonished.

"I can see you don't believe me. That's not good. Where's your faith? Where is the enthusiasm that leads you to rewrite my writings, which tell you nothing, illiterates, copying each letter like children? You should know that what seems evil to us is in fact good; that God, because of our corruption, allows wars, quarrels, infidelities, meanness, robberies, so that hidden evils may come to the surface, where they are consumed and destroyed in their transience. Otherwise, safely hidden in imperishable souls, they would remain eternal. Remember what Martin Luther said: 'Wherever things are better, things are twice as bad there.' The devil is the one who wants peace, who wants serenity, courtesy, and decency; God wants war. He wants disturbance and unrest. He hates the satisfied. Now, I know that you hate my wife and that you get a lot of satisfaction from it, because that hatred maintains your illusion that you love me more. I know you think she's not worthy of me and I deserve a better wife. And I don't blame you for it. She is just as disgusting to me even though I love her. But when a man harmonizes his will with God's, then he clearly sees every diversion he would take if he followed his own desires. I am a debauched man, arrogant and vain, prone to the pleasures, in addition to being a coward. I can clearly see the wide path by which I would have gone to ruin happily singing, if only a miracle had not made me listen to a voice from above and marry Katarina. Then, I would have married Hilde Burkhart. Back then, everyone wanted her. Beautiful girl. Rich. Played the lute. Knew how to read and write. Then no one knew such things, nor do they now, truth is, none of you know; if you ever learn to write and then write about it, write with invisible ink. You can buy it from the alchemist Trebesch. No one knew, I was saying, that Hilde used her reading skills to study godless writings on magic. And, to make matters worse, about fornication magic. Plug your ears as I say this, it's not good for you to hear: with the help of these writings, she was looking for some sort of G-spot hidden in her womb, a point that brings indescribable pleasures, as if the ordinary ones are not fatal enough. Surely, her magic potions and my innate weakness would have led me to depraved experiments. I know for sure—I had a vision—that I would leave the tranquil shoemaking trade and become a merchant. Or something worse. And not just that. You know, children, that Hilde's brother is that unfortunate Fritz, who, to the scandal of honest Christians, converted to Islam and is now called Suleiman Burkhart, and—I can foresee that as well—a foreboding fate awaits him. I am ashamed to admit to you, it's almost as if I did it (because without the intervention of Providence I really would have done it), but I too would have eventually converted to Islam. Because supposedly it is the only truly monotheistic religion that forbids any depiction of images. In fact, it's because its holy book, the Qur'an, looks favorably on bodily pleasures. With trembling in my bones, I have visions that show me in shameful circumstances, because when a person harmonizes his will with God's, he clearly sees all the detours he would take to follow the desires of his own heart. I see myself in a silk robe, with a turban on my head, surrounded by five women, poor peasant women from Westphalia, whom I drag with me off to hell. I watch myself as, disgusting and fat, five times a day I fall to my knees and bow down, thinking that I will thus be saved . . ."

May Master Böhme forgive me for interrupting his God-inspired words, but I cannot resist. Burkhart's conversion to Islam fundamentally shook the peaceful everyday life of the town of Görlitz and announced the arrival of terrible times, described in the books of the prophets and in Revelations. I consider it my duty to describe what happened. As we have already heard, Suleiman Burkhart was a merchant. His work and the devil often took him to Hamburg, Bremen, Linz; he went all the way to distant lands, which possibly don't exist, and from those travels he brought silk, scents, spices, strange stories, and even stranger customs. From one such trip, Burkhart returned on a camel, with a turban on his head and wearing a silk robe. In the square in front of the cathedral, he made the camel kneel, dismounted, took a few steps, and solemnly declared, "Laa ilaaha illalaah, Mohamed ar-Rasool Allah" which in Arabic, if Burkhart pronounced it correctly, is supposed to mean, "There is no God but Allah, and Muhammad is His prophet." Since none of the citizens present knew Arabic, it went unnoticed. But when Burkhart built a mosque in the courtyard of his house, when he converted his servant Wilhelm to Islam, named him Omar, and trained him to call the faithful to prayer five times a day from a narrow tower, which they called a "minaret," things had gone too far. Because some lost souls, poor folk attracted by the free mutton from Suleiman's cauldron, started coming. Pastor Martin Moller, who will be discussed later, visited Burkhart with the intention of diverting him from the wrong path. In vain! The ungodly Suleiman drove him out of the yard like a mangy dog because the poor pastor, in his innocence, entered Burkhart's shrine with his shoes on. The pastor complained to the city councilors. The councilors convened late into the night. And resolved nothing. I mean, nothing good. The merchant Burkhart, they deigned to explain, was bothering no one; his different, though strange, views on God did not concern the worldly authorities; as long as he paid his taxes regularly and obeyed the law, no complaint could be lodged against him. Hearing of the council's decision, Master Böhme turned pale, his forehead drenched in sweat; then he fell into one of those ecstasies in which he had visions. His entire body contorted as he murmured the broken sentences, "Ah, so it begins . . . The separation of church and state . . . The right of people to freely respect the devil is being introduced . . . Early, much sooner than I thought . . ."

The devil does best wherever they think that he does not exist. There it is easiest for him to drive his followers to ruin, to whom he promises gardens of pleasure and rulership of the world. Thus, Suleiman Burkhart followed with great diligence the signposts by which the archfiend marked his wide road, at the end of which the gallows were waiting. Meanwhile, Islam had begun to take root, to attract more and more men and women; three more mosques sprang up; heavy odors and the smells of Eastern spices hovered over Görlitz like the plague. There will be no mention of this in the later chronicles. At least not the official ones. When it was all over, after Burkhart's death, when the Islamic community, bound more by free mutton than faith, disintegrated faster than it had gathered, the mosques and fountains were destroyed, and the city councilors erased from the records any mention of the shameful period of Burkhart's apostasy. But, since nothing can be erased without a trace, the inhabitants of the surrounding towns still mockingly call the people of Görlitz "*Suleimans*" . . .

"That's the fate that would have awaited me if I had obeyed my lust!" continued Master Böhme. And he added, "Remember! Anyone who has a beautiful wife can be sure that he is lost. And if the woman also happens to be cunning and thus succeeds in presenting herself as humble, then her husband is certainly doomed. Protected by the veil of comfortable deception, she will make a cuckold of him, devour his property, and drive him to hell. I assure you, children, our nature is so corrupt that for us the only form of sincere desire for salvation is the constant manifestation of depravity. That is why I am telling you that the hatred that you have begun to feel towards Katarina is useful insofar as you bring it from the depths of your heart into the light of day, but at the same time it is deeply unjust because that lady is an important instrument in my salvation. Her public humiliations and berating bring me a saving serenity. Because, I must be honest with you: if Katarina didn't ridicule me, I could never do it to myself, despite my best intentions. For example, I could never like pigs. And why this is so, I will try to explain to you. Let's go back to that church I mentioned a while ago, the flock is probably still there. Let's hear what the honorable pastor preaches from the pulpit. There he is, shouting, 'You are damned, you carry within you the seed of the original fall from grace.' Fortunately for his salvation, he does not even dream that Adam fell twice. That things with us are twice as bad. For, in the beginning, God created Adam so that he was perfect, without teeth, entrails, and sexual organs, as it is written in Genesis, 'Male and female he created them.' God, therefore, intended to spare us separation and all pain, both in birth and in death. But then a desire was born in Adam. Not from himself, God forbid, it is said that he was created perfect. But Satan, being thrown from the heights into the deepest darkness, felt envy towards Adam, created to dwell in the spiritual world which he had lost forever. It is better for you not to know how that first fall took place, after which the Lord, in order to prevent disobedience from becoming eternal, moved Adam to Eden, which is to say into the transitory world, so that his sin would also become transient and subject to correction. And then, says Genesis, he let a deep sleep fall on Adam and made Eve out of one of his ribs. First of all, to separate from Adam the lust that was to arise in him and thus to place it outside him; then also so that Eve, as an object of his lust, would at the same time be a punishment for it . . ." Here the Master paused. He cleared his throat and said, "I'll tell you the rest some other time. Because, well, here comes Katarina."

Indeed, shortly afterwards, lady Katarina appeared at the door of the workshop, all fragrant and bedecked, in order to confirm the truth of his words with an obvious example. "Jakob, you rogue!" screeched our mistress. "Again, you're preaching to your useless apprentices. That's no surprise. They're the only ones who will listen to you. Respectable folk refuse to listen to your nonsense. Have you forgotten they are burning Hildegard the witch today? Are you planning on not showing up there and incurring wrath on our home and our children? It would not surprise me at all for you to think of an excuse for Hildegard in your fantasies, and to claim that she too will be saved. Immediately go home and clean yourself up as much as possible, you who sleeps with the pigs." Then she turned to us, "And you, run to the cathedral to take a place that befits and suits me." With a heavy heart I recall the scene which followed: starving, hunched over and humiliated, Master Böhme staggered through the yard, and lady Katarina beat him mercilessly with a stick. Caspar even shed a tear. But Otto rebuked him immediately, "Have you forgotten the Master's words so quickly? Be reminded that lady Katarina is an instrument of his and even our own salvation. Because, unless we completely lose our minds, taught by what we have seen and heard, we will never get married. Lady Katarina is our mistress and we are obliged to love her."[6] That is what we did

6. Others' experience is of no help. Later, despite the fact that we swore never to do so, all three of us married, had children, and felt on our own skin the truth of the Master's saying that "a mean wife is more useful for

later, not without resistance. But that is the fate of the mystical path: to love what should naturally be hated; man is never quite clear whether his humility and tranquility are the result of boldly walking the narrow path of salvation or just the most common weakness of character. This, of course, does not apply to the case of Master Böhme; no one denied the correctness of his path, everyone just tried to make it as difficult as possible. And the greater the gifts he received from God, the stronger the pressure of the community. When the master, during his forced stays in the pigsty, learned to speak to the pigs in a mute language, instead of being amazed and rejoicing, people jokingly, and some seriously, invited him to visit their pigs and ask how many piglets to expect. Even the free-spirited pastor Martin Moller, who otherwise supported and protected him, did not like these conversations with animals. It is quite certain that the Master's already great troubles would have been greater if he had not found support in Karl von Eder, a nobleman and eccentric who occasionally thrashed Böhme's tormentors, and who went so far in his mystical ecstasy that he preached a harmonious community of people and animals. Not everything was completely crazy in von Eder's visions. He attributed, for example, most of the evils and misdeeds committed by both humans and animals to the sinister custom of eating meat. He was not alone in that. The alchemist Trebesch thought he was right, but that did not stop him from eating huge quantities of roast kid, or even from sitting at the table of Suleiman Burkhart during the flourishing of Islam in Görlitz. Von Eder, along with Master Böhme, learned to speak the language of pigs fluently, which he considered the most advanced among animal languages, and he even compiled and published an extensive

salvation than ten years of ascetic life in the desert."

German-Swine Dictionary. Perhaps the first dictionary in the history of German linguistics. The dictionary was burned at the stake after some time. In the end, when he went too far and married a cow with the greatest of pomp, von Eder himself was burned. And so, only a handful of ashes remained from that story.

The suspicion that Master Böhme was the protector of witches, which led lady Katarina to cane him so mercilessly, was completely unfounded. I do not know a man who despised witches more than he, and sorcery in general, considering them to be ungodly and worthy of all condemnation by the abuse of the *lumen naturae* that God created for a completely different purpose. Böhme only disapproved of making a spectacle of executions, the desecration of a sacral act, and indulging in base instincts. "Nothing attracts the unrighteous so much as the administration of justice!" he used to say, as a cart with a chained thief in a cage passed by our shop towards the execution site, and the crowd followed behind, shouting insults and curses. Those executions, common at the time, were truly disgusting scenes, though I must admit I enjoyed them. Even today, as an old man, when they burn a witch or behead some sort of father-killer, it is not difficult for me to reach the seventh heaven. But it rarely happens now. Free thinkers, the devil's company, which is getting ever louder, think that it is a sign of the victory of human reason, a consequence of cultivating human nature; but Master Böhme, predicting the arrival of the atheistic period of enlightenment, thinks differently and sees in this indulgence a weakening sense of justice. He believes that a secret lawlessness is gaining momentum. That the ruler of this world is growing stronger. He went so far as to foresee the arrival of such times in which, not only will witches not be burned at all, they will do whatever they want unhindered. He supports my predisposition to observe executions. "Look, Schwenekpfeld," he tells me. "You could overcome it. Pretend that it doesn't interest you. But it is better for you to go and enjoy the tortuous scenes, because otherwise vanity will overwhelm you, you will not get rid of your sinful inclinations, and you will be harmed because of it. So, go there, indulge in the forces that be, you will pay dearly for it anyway. But you have no other choice.

"Because everyone suffers as much humiliation as he wishes for glory, and everyone suffers exactly as much as he indulges in pleasures."

2

On the day when the witch Hildegard was burned after many awkward and tortuous scenes, Böhme was in a state of special inspiration. The day itself was somehow foreboding. It rained all morning, and then a thick fog rose from the swamp around the Neisse. Otto and Caspar carried a litter with lady Katarina; behind them, holding my hand, walked Böhme. I have never seen such a thick fog before or since. In vain, I peered about, trying to see something. "Schwenekpfeld, you godless idiot!" said the Master, seeing my fear. "With so little faith, how will you ever walk on water? Listen carefully! I will say the words the Spirit speaks to me. We will follow His words and surely reach the stake where, although we deserve it, we will not burn this time: *We have the clear example of Lucifer, and also of Adam, to testify to what selfishness does when it catches the light of nature and when it appropriates it. We also see people skilled in the sciences, that when their minds possess the lumen naturae nothing else arises from it but pride in themselves. But, be careful! While reason is trapped and firmly bound in God's wrath and in its own earthliness, it is very dangerous to use the lumen naturae if it is possessed by selfishness . . ."* There is no need to quote further because following the God-inspired words we came to the square, and the text is preserved in my transcript, available to all who hunger for wisdom, even though the Master later ate it with delight. But many were unlucky that day. The coppersmith Reinhart fell into a ditch and broke both legs; some women went astray and went all the way to Bautzen, where there was also fog. They took the best seats in the square in Bautzen and waited for the arrival of the procession of city councilors, judges, and guards. In the end, when it was completely dark, they realized that something was wrong, that there would be no execution, but then it was too late. The city guards picked them up and beat them for vagrancy. Rightly so! That, however, was not the end of the confusion. The esteemed Lady Hedwig von Clausewitz had set out with her companion for Hildegard's execution; along the way, as women will do, they talked about anything and everything, which would not have been of consequence if, quite by accident, Lady Hedwig's husband, Arnim von Clausewitz, had not stumbled upon them. He did not see them, but, being in their immediate vicinity, he recognized his wife's voice. He must have been astonished when he heard from the mouth of the woman with whom he had shared vows and exalted up until yesterday that he was a scoundrel, a cuckold, and a miser; that his mouth stinks worse than his feet, and that Mrs. Hedwig had been, for three years, the mistress of the Görlitz doctor Herbert Mayer who had been a family friend, and whose lovemaking skills the lady spoke of with great respect. Von Clausewitz acted as honor dictates: he beat his wife to death with a stick. Again, rightly so. However, in the low visibility, instead of Hedwig, he beat her seemingly innocent companion, breaking her nose and four ribs. Later, however, already during the reading of Hildegard's verdict and the enumeration of the crimes she committed, it became known that her companion Ingrid had been justly punished; Mayer had enchanted and conquered Lady Hedwig with the help of Hildegard's magic potions; Ingrid had taken part in the devil's work by secretly pouring a potion into the lady's wine.

News of these events, magnified a hundredfold, spread throughout the city of Görlitz like the plague. Men and women, gathered in cliques, carefully crossed themselves, spitting for protection against the spells, and commenting on the events. Sinful curiosity also led me to go from group to group, to listen to what is being said, and to enjoy the miraculous twists in the story. But not for long. Master Böhme quickly caught up with me, beat me about the head with his staff, and said, "Schwenekpfeld, you rascal, you are quick to hear evil. Listen to what I'm about to say. Heed my words well. Nothing is as it seems. Especially nothing that the common folk think it is. Here, you hear them say that Reinhard was justly punished, because they say that he incurred God's wrath by constantly cursing his father. Far from it! This is actually how the honorable Reinhard obtained God's grace. And it was this grace that led him to fall into the ditch, to become crippled and thus avoid the two great evils that would otherwise befall him. If, following his will, he had come here, the painful circumstances that we all witnessed would have embarrassed him and made him get drunk in the infamous *The Three-legged Swine* tavern. I know what you're thinking, 'How strange that he would want to get drunk.' The problem is not inebriation. But that drunkenness would be used by the prostitute Jolka to seduce the coppersmith, which would do great harm to his honest soul. Then comes the second evil: Reinhardt intends to travel to Weimar on business. If he had not been struck by this so-called accident, he would have set off next week and arrived just in time to lose his life in the attack of the Swedes, who will devastate the city. Here, you see, Schwenekpfeld, how Providence works and how it protects us wisely from our own delusions.

"Further, Schwenekpfeld. Now everyone is cursing Ingrid and praising the virtue of Lady Hedwig. And everyone is firmly convinced that a vile fraud has been exposed. Our reason, however, as well as our senses, constantly leads us to the wrong conclusions; the unfortunate Ingrid did secretly pour the potion into Lady Hedwig's wine, but with the best of intentions, deceived by the doctor's lie that the potion was in fact a tonic for improving her circulation. It is true, then, that Lady Hedwig was led by a magic potion to commit a lewd sin with Mayer—how would she otherwise have slept with such an ugly old man—but it is also true that, without the influence of any magic potion, she has been Baron von Kinsky's mistress for years. Von Clausewitz also knows this, but he does not dare to do anything because he owes von Kinsky a large sum of money, and he is also afraid, quite justifiably, that the baron will kill him if he objects at all. However, a just punishment hangs over Hedwig's head; it just hasn't happened to her yet. You will see, as soon as the executioner brings the torch to the stake, lady Hedwig will be covered with disgusting ulcers that will completely destroy her ungodly beauty. As for those two cacklers who mistakenly wandered off to Bautzen, they simply deserved to be beaten for their petty sins; so since their husbands were sissies, the Finger of God took them to another city to be whipped in order to balance the sin and suffering in the Saxon principality."

The crowd was already at the peak of impatience when, clad in a dignified black toga, the city councilor Küchenmeister appeared, who had Latinized his surname into Archimagrius out of vanity. The esteemed counselor pompously ordered that the convicted be brought out. The guards quickly descended into the dungeon for Hildegard and returned even faster from below. Something had gone wrong. The commander of the guard whispered something in the ear of the city councilor; Councilor Archimagrius became enraged, threw the scrolls into the mud in anger, and began to shout, "Tie them up! Bring them here! They'll pay for this." And here's what had happened. The jailers, the three of them, thought of making the time pass by fornicating with the witch; there was also some wine and sausage—a real satanic orgy. The guards struggled to separate the intertwined bodies, to find Hildegard among them—who, like the jailers, had her head shaved—to tie her up, and take them all out onto the square. Hildegard's execution was to be the culmination of a whole series of verdicts. According to the custom and law of the time, a number of animals awaiting punishment were among the villains. That is how Johann Fischer's boar, which was proven to have bitten Frau Sitzfleisch by the buttocks, was sentenced to be buried alive. The punishment, despite the loud protests of the great von Eder, was carried out immediately. It was the turn of Elsa the cow, owned by Joachim Lemerschwanz, caught for the third time in a neighbor's cabbage field, which was sentenced to one hundred blows with a club. Surprisingly, von Eder did not object, although he would later, with a darkened mind, marry Elsa's own sister. And that punishment was carried out. Night was approaching, so Councilor Archimagrius decided to abandon the protocol and to cut off the hands of thieves, singe the beards off perjurers, and cut off the ears of slanderers all at the same time, in a shortened procedure, without reading the verdicts; this led to indescribable confusion, in which several culprits got away and fled the execution site, while some innocent bystanders were mistakenly left without hands and beards. Blood all around, wails of pain, vain cries for mercy! Not a trace of that organization, pedantry, and discipline which, if Böhme's predictions are to be believed, will be a characteristic feature of future generations of Germans, serving as both their superiority and their curse.

Only when, to the shame of the pedantic descendants, the general insubordination and commotion somehow subsided, was Hildegard tied to the stake. The crowd went silent. Lady Katarina fainted. Several other women followed her example. The executioner put the torch to the firewood. I looked Lady Hedwig up and down to see if she was getting purulent sores. But nothing happened. The lady didn't get sores, nor did the firewood, soaked by the rain, catch fire. This encouraged Hildegard. "You peasants!" she cried. "And yet it moves!" These words left no impression. "The earth is turning, you fools! It's round, as round as Küchenmeister's head, and it's spinning like a top." Now this had terrible consequences. Ladies fainted. I became nauseated and dizzy. The ground quaked beneath my feet. Many otherwise virtuous husbands, were shocked and started vomiting. The honorable pastor Martin Moller, pale as a ghost, staggering, somehow climbed to the balcony of the Magistrate and began to calm the citizens from above. "Have you completely lost your minds?" he thundered like a prophet. "Have you sold your souls to Hildegard's master, the devil? Nothing has changed! The earth is still flat. Everything is still in its place. Just look around yourselves." The pastor's determination affected the naivety of the simple folk, and balance was immediately restored. But Hildegard wasn't giving in. "My ass, sure, the Earth is flat! And you know it very well, pastor!" I must admit, the devil's companion was right there. At that time, the learned people in Görlitz already knew about the teachings of Nicolaus Copernicus, although they could not quite get used to him because it made them dizzy.

Nevertheless, since the spherical shape of the Earth and its rotation around its own axis did not contradict the Gospels in any way, the teaching was accepted, but out of caution it was kept as a secret of state. It will remain unclear how Hildegard, ignorant as she was, found out; the devil must have whispered it to her, the Father of Lies, who sometimes does not lie. Just as holy men, like Master Böhme, so as not to become too exalted, sometimes agree with him.

Archimagrius, meanwhile, ordered the servants to bring some tar. Red-faced and rolling his eyes, the magistrate began to read the long list of Hildegard's crimes. Men and women, honorable citizens and gentle ladies, seemed to be offended by listening to the enumeration of the iniquities committed by the witch; in fact, they were enjoying themselves. I know, because I was enjoying it myself. After all, such occasions serve to make honest people listen to everything that they must not even think about, but which they still carry deeply woven into their hearts. Hildegard, on the other hand, as if not staring death in the face, didn't shut her mouth. "It's true!" she screamed from the stake. "I was the devil's concubine. And not just one devil, but three of them. And I'm not the least bit ashamed. At least I lived my life to the full. But the way you poor bastards . . . (here, Hildegard used a verb that cannot be repeated out of decency), soon all of your wives will sit on the devil's . . . (again, an indecent word)." This could no longer be tolerated. Archimagrius ordered that the witch be silenced. The servants stuffed her mouth with clay, but to everyone's dismay, with a slightly squeakier but equally toxic voice, Hildegard then spoke through her rear end. "Nothing can help you, you culinary bastard," she hissed at Archimagrius. "Even if you stuff all the mud of Saxony in my mouth, I will right here and now from the proper place, let them all know that you didn't manage to put your thing in me, even though you begged and tried, and drank in vain the tinctures that the alchemist Trebesch sold you for a lot of money. I'm not afraid of your silly fire, which you can't even light; I can't wait to let my soul go through my ass, to go down to where my master is impatiently waiting for me, and to never see your miserable and dejected faces again."

Then the servants brought barrels of tar. "Don't hold back!" screamed Archimagrius, blue in the face from anger. And by God they didn't. They even overdid it. In their zeal, they smeared a lot of tar on themselves as well. So the fire, when they lit the stake again, also caught Archimagrius's boyfriend, one-eyed Ludwig, who, instead of lying on the ground and waiting to be put out with robes, rags and coats, panicked and ran, as if he could escape death. It was a fatal mistake. There could have been a few quick-footed lads who could catch up with him and put out the flames, but no one wanted to leave the execution site just at the moment when the spectacle had begun, so they left Ludwig to his fate. And fate led him, all on fire, to the artisans' street, where most of the houses were made of wood. In agony, Ludwig ran hither and thither, running into walls, bouncing off, crossing from side to side, and quickly spreading the fire like a blazing plague that punished some of those who did not come to his aid, leaving them without a roof over their heads. God punished the others later, each in his own way.

And as if out of spite, stifled by the thick smoke of the green wood, the fire at the stake was barely smoldering. It was already getting dark; something urgent had to be done to save the now shaky authority of the Magistrate. Having no other recourse, Archimagrius ordered the servants to quickly bring the bellows from the smithies and to set the fire ablaze like real men. The bellows did in fact help, but before they were used, confusion rose again. The head of the blacksmith's guild, a certain Joachim, opposed the intention to fan the flames with their bellows. He claimed that the bellows would be defiled in that way, that they would absorb the breath of ruin, which would inevitably result in a lower quality of axes, sickles, and horseshoes. Already completely out of his mind, Archimagrius punished him on the spot with fifty lashes on the ass. He punished the blacksmiths who supported him in the rebellion with twenty-five each. And the apprentices, who did nothing and who were quieter than mice, got twenty each, just because they were apprentices. All the while, behind an opaque curtain of smoke, Hildegard laughed wickedly. Until finally, the raging fire silenced her. And when the wood had burned out, when the smoke dissipated, it was found with apprehension that all the flames did not do much harm to the witch. True, she was dead, or pretending to be, but apart from her clothes, hair and pubic hair, her body was almost intact, only here and there slightly tanned and flushed. The servants hurriedly removed the corpse from the stake and threw it into a previously dug pit under the Cursed Oak, the tree where the ungodly committed suicide. And then they quickly filled the hole with wet soil.

In all the confusion, some thieves from Karlovy Vary saw the greatest benefit, having, due to a multitude of extraordinary circumstances, been completely forgotten. Human justice is imperfect, our memory is short. No one even noticed that they had escaped. They were never mentioned again. I don't even know how I remembered them. That, however, was far from the end of the unrest that day. As if it wasn't enough that a whole street burned down due to haste and clumsiness, that Ludwig, the reluctant arsonist, burned up with it; as if it were a small thing that a few honest blacksmiths were whipped and disgraced within an inch of their lives, defending the rights of their guild; not to mention the broken legs and fear suffered; as if all this were not enough, at the moment when the crowd began to dissipate, Johannes Schneider, the tailor, or in the new Latin fashion, Sartorius, found it appropriate to turn on Master Böhme. And for what reason? Because of a superfluous, if it was superfluous at all, letter "S." "Honorable citizens of Görlitz!" cried Sartorius from the balcony of the Magistrate. "Hold on for a moment." Although frozen and in a bad mood, the men stopped because the voice came from the building where the earthly government resided. The women went on home; the time had not come for them to meddle in politics. There was still a sense of order. Although not for long. "You may be wondering, citizens," Sartorius continued, "why the things are happening to us that we witnessed today. You must be questioning and answering in your honest hearts that it is all the devil's workings. In that, you are completely right. But the devil, as a spiritual being without external organs, is unable to realize his intentions on his own; his limbs and tools are our fellow citizens, people like you and me, who help him wholeheartedly. That help does not always have to be of the kind provided to the archfiend by the recently burned Hildegard, that is, out in the open. There are those among us who pave the way for Satan in a subtle way, imperceptibly changing old and good customs, introducing tempting innovations and thus creating instability suitable for all sorts of evil. Here, for example, we have the shoemaker Böhme. The general opinion is that, although a little bit strange, he is a good Christian, craftsman, and husband, but believe it or not, he writes the name of one of his apprentices, Caspar, with two 'S's' instead of one (Casspar); he thus exalts his servant above all other, numerous and praiseworthy Caspars, who, like their ancestors, write their name as it has been written since time immemorial."

"Is it possible?!" "Unheard of!" "He was always suspicious to me!" were the comments heard among the crowd. Seeing that it had caused a favorable effect, Sartorius continued with his deceitful rhetoric. "Moreover, fellow citizens, he writes his own surname in several different ways. Once *Boehme,* another time *Boehmen,* and then *Bome, Bohme,* even *Beeme.* What kind of man is he, who doesn't know, or doesn't want to know, what his own last name is? It is incomprehensible contempt for his ancestors. Although his ancestors certainly deserve that contempt, such an attitude towards tradition cannot be allowed . . ."[7]

The crowd stirred, always ready to behead someone. There were already whispers that the desecrator of the letter S should be tied to the stake; at any moment the whispers could turn into shouts, and at that time, the distance from shouts to the stake was only a few steps. I looked at the Master. He was utterly calm. Even more, absent. In the abyss of his pristine inner workings. "He knows it's not his time yet," I thought. And I was right. That is, he was right; he was calm, and my knees were knocking, not so much for fear for the master's life as for my own; for, I have just described the perverse custom, that under Saxon law apprentices, whether or not involved in the guilt, must suffer the same punishment as their master. I can't say for sure how things would have gone, certainly not well for the master and me, if von Eder hadn't materialized from somewhere. Furious at what he thought was the barbaric punishment of innocent animals, angry at Sartorius over some earlier disputes, appalled

7. We cannot know for certain whether the old dispute in orthography held in front of the Magistrate's building in Görlitz had any influence on the change in the writing of the name Caspar, but insight into the written documents indicates that the name, all the way up until the mid-seventeenth century, was written with two S's. Since then, as time has passed the double S is encountered less and less, and since the beginning of the eighteenth century, the name Caspar has been written with just one S. (editor's note)

at the senseless accusations against Master Böhme, von Eder climbed onto the Magistrate's balcony, caught up with Sartorius, who tried to escape and, using the *ius primae noctis,* beat him mercilessly in front of everyone present. (Just to remove all doubt, I am obliged to explain how, on the basis of the *ius primae noctis,* the great von Eder had the right to beat a city councilor, a highly respected and wealthy man. Sartorius's grandfather Frederick was the tailor of von Eder's father. Both Sartorius's father and Sartorius were born in the count's castle; consequently, they were his subjects and were also obliged to offer their bride to the nobleman after the wedding. Over time this right ceased to be exercised; instead of taking the bride's virginity, they were satisfied to beat the groom, after giving him valuable lessons on married life. And then this custom faded as well. But von Eder still had the right, and no one could object.) Much less could he be objected to for protecting the Master from unfounded accusations. We know the Germans still had no dictionary. Or grammar. Not to mention orthography and spelling. How could he be blamed for spelling Caspar's name with two S's, even though I no longer dare to? But, hand on my heart, I have to admit that the Master fiddled with the language a lot. In his rare moments of leisure, he had the custom of coming up with new words. I randomly remember some of them: *Flugzeug, Tonkatuigerat, Dasein, Plattenspieler* . . . and many others which still mean nothing, but which will take on meaning sometime in the future.

Here is a real example of what kind of man Master Jakob Böhme was. As von Eder whipped Sartorius, even though the man had worked insidiously to remove the Master's head, tears of pity and sympathy for the counselor's humiliation and pain trickled down his face. When the flogging was over, the Master began to lament that Sartorius's plan had been thwarted, and that we had been spared burning at the stake. “Schwenekpfeld,” he sobbed, “nothing purifies like the flames of the stake. I don’t know why that is. But it’s true. Especially if a man is unjustly condemned and burned, his bliss is indescribable.” To be honest, I was not at all sorry that we were let off, so I hurried to get the master as far away from the square as possible, before anyone remembered that Otto’s name was written with two T’s. The fog had lifted, but the night was moonless; once again nothing could be seen. However, we easily found our way by following the traces that the Master’s words had left in the air. The devil did not give me peace, I could not stop myself from saying, “Today you prophesied that with the first flame the face and body of lady Hedwig would break out with disgusting ulcers, but nothing happened.” “Who says that nothing happened?” the Master replied. “How do you know that nothing happened? Just because you didn’t see anything does not mean that something didn’t happen. The eyes are unreliable. Not everything is visible at the moment it happens. Be patient. These days we will be visited by the homunculus Cohausen, the messenger of the Philosopher of the Monarchy, the Prince of the Spagirists, the Chief Astronomer, the Unsurpassed Physician and the Trismegistus of mechanical arcana, Bombast Paracelsus. Cohausen is bringing the latest writings of the learned doctor about the true nature of various diseases. When I have read them, I will tell you what happened. But now,” the Master ordered, “let’s drop by the house of the coppersmith Reinhard, because our duty requires us to visit a neighbor and a friend who is in great pain.”

Indeed, the poor cooper was lying in bed, all gray in the face, but in good spirits. Seeing Master Böhme, he was even more excited. “The Lord Himself brings you, Jakob,” he said. “Praise be to the day I broke my legs; it is known that when you visit the sick, you speak most inspiringly, so I hope that tonight I’ll have the chance to hear something useful for the soul. And, to be honest, an honest man doesn't need legs." Reinhard's youngest daughter, Wilhelmina (who would later become my wife), brought a jug of schnapps and poured us a glass. And Master Böhme immediately delighted us with his unparalleled candor. "My dear Reinhard," he said, "I will be honest with you! I came to visit you tonight because I'm afraid to go home. Katarina is angry that I always find apprentices whose names have double consonants. What worries me the least is that I will spend the night in the barn, with the pigs. But I'm sure she'll scold me until she falls asleep, so I selfishly decided to visit you and put off the inconvenience for later. I would certainly visit you tomorrow, but I want you to know the whole truth." Then he added, "It is true that I speak most inspiringly at the bedside of the infirm, and that is nothing strange. Didn't the Lord say to Paul, *my strength is made perfect in weakness*. And that is why tonight I will tell you about the saving weakness of our Lord Jesus Christ, while I still can; the days are coming when that will no longer be possible . . ."

We were all ears. The chickens and pigs fell silent that had been squirming and grunting in the corner intended for animals in Reinhard's house.

"You know, my dear ones," the Master began to narrate, "how great is the mystery of the birth of our Lord Jesus Christ. Since the world was created from nothing, and from the matter of that world, further, man was created, decay and death are immanent to all of creation from the beginning. Pay no heed, my children, to the sermons that teach that the Lord punished Adam. Not at all. God punished no one. And He did not threaten Adam, but rather warned him, '*thou shalt not eat of it: for in the day that thou eatest thereof thou shalt surely die.*' Did not Adam weep bitterly, seeing what he had done? Does not God forgive all who repent? He would have forgiven Adam. But, the seed of death, as I already said, was in Adam and in Eden; the Son of God would have been born as a man, even if Adam had not sinned, because it was the only way for death to be removed from the human body, and then through man from nature itself as well. But that incarnation was supposed to take place in glory and light, and not in shame and suffering. In His divine wisdom, the Lord arranged it so that the very consequences of sin, shame, and suffering have become the steps of redemption. That is why, my dear ones, all shame and all suffering is precious. Be ashamed, suffer, and rejoice! Observe the life of the Lord Jesus Christ and do as he did. Go unnoticed! Remain silent! Do your job well. Think not of yourself. You can do nothing for your salvation. Get out of your own way, forget everything that can be forgotten. God will do everything for you, you clumsy bastard . . .

"And remember his way. The last night of his earthly life. He knew he was to die, no comfort anywhere to be found. His disciples were sleeping. Judas was counting his pieces of silver. He knew that he was God, but his Divine hypostasis was of no help to him; God could not help man without killing him, even when He Himself became man. So, unable and unwilling to share the suffering of the cross, His hypostasis of God withdrew and only the carpenter Jesus remained in the Garden of Gethsemane. That separation from oneself, that incomprehensible abandonment of oneself, that sacrifice that transcends all reason, overthrew the insignificance of Adam's separation from God, and death was already destroyed; all that remained was to die. Knowing that he created the world and the people who were to crucify him, he calmly endured humiliation, suffering and—the worst of all evils—death. Although he knew he would be resurrected on the third day, the bitterness of dying was no less. Now pay attention! One robber was crucified on both sides of the Lord's cross. Both men steeped in evil. They killed, robbed, and raped. Their evil deeds were the same or almost the same. Perhaps the deeds of the one on the right, the one who would be saved, were even worse. Quite certainly they were worse. They were so horrible that even a dead robber's conscience was no longer able to bear them, and he begged Jesus to forgive him. And the Lord forgave him. My sons, I want you to keep that in mind all the time: all of us, each and every one of us, is worse than those two thieves. Because the world is getting worse every day, and a lot of time has passed since then. I want you to never forget: our works cannot save us; they are all abominable, every last one. Only a heartfelt plea for God's mercy can save us . . ."

3

In the middle of 1625, Master Böhme decided to stop sleeping. He no longer ate the little servings of paper that were keeping him alive. I was happy and sad at the same time; happy that some of his writings would be preserved (although he managed to eat the best ones), unhappy because it was clear that his earthly days were numbered. Caspar and Otto moved to Bremen. And two painful events took place, one of which confirmed the power of Böhme's spiritual contemplation, and the other proved the fatality of leaving the saving auspices of faith. Namely, in just one day, lady Hedwig first contracted disgusting ulcers and then died in the most horrible torment, and Suleiman Burkhart, the merchant who converted to Islam, was hanged. And it was high time someone was hanged. Since the burning of the witch Hildegard, there had been no mention of noteworthy events, and melancholy had been hovering over Görlitz, threatening to cause an epidemic of suicides.

Blood must be spilt from time to time. But not the blood of thieves, the price must be paid with the blood of honorable people.

But I had better start from the beginning. For those who have forgotten lady Hedwig, she was that disobedient and unfaithful woman whom the master prophesied would be covered with ulcers the moment the executioner brought the torch to the stake of the witch Hildegard. In her rudeness, the lady dared to not fulfill Böhme's prediction—of course only from the outside—which shook me, ignorant and stupid, and my confidence in the Master. In fact, as it turned out, she instantly burst into festering sores from within; accustomed, however, to concealing shameful secrets, which will later be called the *incubation period,* she somehow managed to keep them under her skin. Only then did I understand why Böhme kept repeating to us, "Whatever you do, don't keep secrets. Because after a while, they are not secrets kept from others, but from yourself as well. It's better for you to go out on the main town square in the middle of the day and open your hearts to everyone —in the worst case they will consider you to be fools, which you are—rather than let the secrets strengthen inside you, suck your blood, and finally, when they gain independence, come out into the light of day and testify against you as diseases."

And that's exactly what happened to lady Hedwig. That morning —it was learned later from the stories of her servant Fatima, the seventh wife of Suleiman Burkhart—everything seemed normal. Lady Hedwig got out of bed and, as usual, sat in front of the mirror to rub balsams on herself. First, said Fatima, she noticed a very small pimple on her forehead, and that pimple caused the lady such an outburst of anger that she pinched the unfortunate spot till it was bloody. Her wrath only accelerated the processes of sinful decay. Soon the pimple was the size of a hazelnut, and then reached the size of a walnut, and finally a hen's egg. The constraints of the written medium do not allow the descriptions of the accelerated growth of the purulent sores which were accompanied by the eerie cries of lady Hedwig in real time, so they come here with a delay, like an echo. These cries, on the other hand, did not provoke any reaction in the neighborhood either. Namely, they were an everyday occurrence, only they were usually the product of the lady's daily indulgences in debauchery. Either with a maid, or with one of her lovers (whose names I don't mention because those gentlemen think they are honorable), or even with all of them at the same time. Our lady's husband, Arnim von Clausewitz, had been on a business trip to Bavaria for seven years, although he had no business there, and actually spent most of that time in Görlitz. That business trip was just an elegant excuse for an honest man not to be present for his wife's indescribable misdeeds.

All in all, there was no help in sight. That's the way it is in sinful relationships. Everyone is around in the days of pleasure, not a trace to be found of them in the days of hellish torture. "Run and get Dr. Rilke! Run and get Dr. Rilke!" screamed lady Hedwig as the ulcers spread all over her body, bursting and releasing a fetid mixture of blood and pus. Fatima, in a panic, set off in search of him. As if out of spite, Dr. Rilke, who all the time, idle and ambitious, was hanging about this story, standing on his tiptoes and peeking over the crowd so that I would not notice and mention him; that day he seemed to have sunk into the earth. In the end, the servant Fatima found him drunk as a skunk in the *Seven Dull Knives* tavern. Somehow the two of them, Rilke and Fatima, stumbled (while convincing the doctor of the urgency of the case, Fatima also drank some schnapps) to Hedwig's house, but it was all too late. Of the lady whose beauty had taken away the breath of noble husbands, only a puddle of sticky black liquid remained, which pulsed for some time and gave signs of some sort of primitive life, until it finally went still completely.

As soon as the pious people poured the remains of lady Hedwig into a larger jar and started throwing it in the Cursed Hole,[8] not far from the Cursed Oak (the priest forbade the deceased to be buried in a liquid state in the cemetery), the news spread through Görlitz that the merchant Suleiman Burkhart was to be hanged in the afternoon. And here's what had happened: Burkhart was caught at the moment when he was stuffing a string of pork sausages down his pants. If he had not converted to Islam, if he had remained under the auspices of his ancestral faith, he would have been punished much more lightly. In the worst case, they would cut off his right hand or singe his beard. But, that's the way times were. Non-believers were looked down upon, the hand of justice was heavier, and the city councilors had no mercy: death by hanging. The aggravating circumstance was the fact that the sausages contained pork. Since Islam forbids the use of that meat, the advisers were of the opinion that Burkhart was so incorrigible and ungodly that he did not respect even the dogmas of his newly adopted religion.

The hanging was scheduled for six o'clock.

Of course, that was a big day for Katarina, Böhme's wife-teacher. That woman didn't miss a single hanging, a single burning, and especially not a beheading, but—no matter how bad she actually was—I didn't take it as a bad thing because those occasions were nice little

8. This will one day be called a "footnote." It will be forgotten that this is my invention. So, the Cursed Hole is the place where all the useless things were thrown from the environs of Görlitz (there weren't many of them, in those days almost everything that existed was needed). But among those things there were strange ones, like this slip of paper which the gravedigger Manfred found: ( )

festivities for me as well. Even Böhme himself approved of attending executions, for instructive reasons, believing that it is good for people to watch such scenes so as not to forget the existence of death. To which sinful human nature is quite prone. Lady Katarina burst into the workshop somehow politely and gave us the news. "Did you hear, Jakob," screeched the busybody, "that the whore Hedwig completely disintegrated and turned into resin?" Böhme kept his mouth shut. I kept mine even more shut. But I couldn't help but imagine the surface of the stinking puddle that would have been left behind by lady Katarina if only she were, not a beauty, but at least less of an eyesore. Because only Böhme could love her. Because lady Katarina's honor rested on rotten foundations. No one wanted to even look at her. Much the less do other things. But lady Hedwig, apart from having an increased libido (does this word already exist in the non-existent Dictionary of the German Language?) and endless vanity like all women, was a very dear person. "What do you think, Jacob," muttered our mistress, "is the adulteress already in hell? Have her tortures already begun? Is she already repenting in vain for everything she did?"

Master Böhme put down his work, and pronounced a horrible heresy, "Hell doesn't exist." Horrified, lady Katarina quickly plugged her ears, trying to give the impression that she didn't really hear anything, because in those days one could still end up on the stake if they only dared to hear a heresy, regardless of whether they agreed with, or even opposed it. I, for my part, no less horrified, drove a nail into a finger on my left hand, instead of into a sole, and let out a terrible scream. Paying no heed to that, however, Böhme picked up his work again and repeated, "Yes, it is so! Hell doesn't exist."

"Good Lord, who did I marry? I, who was offered proposals from the handsomest lads in Saxony and Selisia," whimpered

Katarina. "You bastard, do you want me to be burned at the stake because I heard what I didn't actually hear? And not only did I not hear it, but I was not even here when you uttered what you uttered in your madness. See, I just now came in. And I wouldn't even have come in if I didn't need to forbid you two to think I was coming to the workshop." Having said that, she vanished even more quickly than she had appeared. Then Master Böhme smiled and said, "Pull that nail out of your finger and listen to what I say!"

I trembled like a reed listening to my teacher's sublime words. "Yes, Schwenekpfeld, hell does not exist. But it's not useful for people to know that. Do you see all the evil and wickedness in the world? Just imagine what it would look like if people knew that everyone will be saved. The concept of hell is what keeps this world from turning into hell. However, that does not mean that everyone will be comfortable in heaven. Far from it. God rejects no one, and all are invited to eternal life. However, some do not want to accept the abundant outpouring of life. That's just the way it is. Put a good man in hell, and even there he'll be happy and he'll even find meaning. Take a reprobate to heaven, and he'll find it to be confining and unbearable. But now go, put on your best clothes, it's time for us to get down to the town square. Soon they will hang the unfortunate Burkhart."

It's well-known that Böhme especially enjoyed teaching while going to an execution. In the good old days, burnings and hangings were fairly frequent, and as a consequence, Caspar, Otto, and I received an admirable theological education. This time, due to the teacher's malnutrition and exhaustion, the trip to the town square took a long time, so there was plenty of time to talk. "Food, my son!" Böhme whispered. "Food is the root of all evil in this world. Remember it well. I have known many, otherwise honorable people, who were driven to ruin by a weakness towards their stomachs. Too much food creates black bile, black bile, then, causes melancholy; melancholy, in turn, oppresses the soul, which ceases to believe in the possibility of salvation and indulges in pointless fantasies. Here's an example. I knew a tanner named Gerhard, a great glutton, whom the devil convinced that he was in fact a clay jar. Fearing that he would break, he completely neglected his job and sat in the house all day. But destiny brought about by imagination cannot be escaped. On one occasion, he went out into the yard, tripped over a rake, and was smashed into smithereens. That's how strong the imagination is. It can turn you into an angel, but also into a chair. I say unto you, whoever eats a lot of pork, he shall not eat of the Tree of Life. And now listen and remember, because I will not be writing any longer . . ."

Through the power of imagination I became all ears, and Böhme went on preaching.

"Hark unto me! For whoever wants to be saved and receive eternal life, the real danger begins at the moment when gourmandizing is the victor. Such a man is then faced with an even greater danger: with the demons of thinking and reflecting. For a mystic, there is no greater peril than thinking. No matter how sublime and beatific it might be. But before we begin elaborating on that, we should go back to the beginning. Because time began at the moment of the Fall. It is important to know that our nature is not corrupt, as the fanatical priests teach, but that it does not exist at all. We have no nature whatsoever. Our lives are counterfeits. It is also important to know that Adam's disobedience interrupted the Creation process. It is correct that everything the Lord created was *very good*. But it was not yet *perfect*. Heaven, earth, plants, animals, and man were still just vessels that the Lord needed to fill, using Adam as a mysterious funnel, with his eternal life. The Tree of Knowledge of Good and Evil and the Tree of Life stood next to each other, but of course, not like two trees standing in one of our earthly orchards. Adam was supposed to eat first from the Tree of Life, and only then from the Tree of Knowledge of Good and Evil; but the impatience from which we all suffer terribly made him, trusting in himself, deaf to the order of things. The result was a twofold mistake: he lost his life, and he did not receive knowledge."

Executions in Görlitz were, as a rule, sloppy. We were still far from the Teutonic pedantry that our descendants will one day be proud of. It often happened that a completely innocent passerby was executed, and the real culprit escaped with impunity. Just remember the confusion that occurred during the execution of the witch Hildegard. This time, the city councilors took all measures to reduce the riots and bedlam to a minimum. But Görlitz would not be Görlitz if everything ran smoothly. That's the way it was with Suleiman Burkhart's hanging. At the beginning, it seemed that everything would be all right. Burkhart calmly listened to the verdict and then said contemptuously, "Big deal. Death is much better than life among the heathen in this fleabag town." He used his right to a last wish: he had them bring the sausages, which the infidel then ecstatically ate. Then the drum roll was heard and the executioner kicked the chair away. To his own misfortune. Because he had accidentally, incomprehensibly for such an experienced executioner, hurriedly placed the noose around his own neck instead of Burkhart's. He noticed it too late, when the noose tightened and began to choke him, but he somehow managed by gestures (the precursors to sign language) to send a message: help! The police ran up, twenty-two of them, all at once, which led to an indescribable commotion under the scaffold and also to the next fatal mistake:

instead of cutting the rope, one of the lads cut off the misfortunate executioner's head. All of that made Burkhart abnormally happy, and he shouted, "Jihad! Jihad!"

What was he so happy about? The rope was prepared once again, and the crowd present managed to warn the executioner's assistant in time to pull the noose around Suleiman's neck and not around his own, because he, all confused and shaken, had repeated his teacher's mistake. Or perhaps he did it intentionally. It's possible that he was just blindly loyal to his teacher and was just following his example. Just as once the three of us apprentices, when Master Böhme accidentally drove a nail into his finger, did the same, thinking that it was part of the craft. Again the drum roll! Again the chair was kicked away. And what happened? Burkhart plunged into the hole. But, instead of stopping abruptly and having his neck broken, the clever infidel fell into the earth. The ground closed up over him. The only evidence of the hanging was just the broken rope, swaying gently in the evening breeze. This was immediately interpreted as a bad sign. As if other signs exist besides bad ones. The crowd became unruly. In order to stop the commotion, Councilman Archimagrius climbed onto the gallows and solemnly announced, "Burkhart was so sinful that God sent him straight to hell."

"All right, Schwenekpfeld!" said Master Böhme. "This is also over. We can go home now." And so, on the way from the execution site to the workshop, the famous *A Dialogue between a Scholar and His Master about Where the Blessed and the Damned Souls Go When They Depart from Their Bodies* came about. Although it was, in fact, more like a monologue. Dull-witted and chatty as I am, I asked Böhme, "What do you think, master, has Suleiman Burkhart's soul already reached hell?" But Böhme said, "Remember what I'm about to say, and write it down later. Burkhart's soul did not go to hell. It was already in hell. And the same thing happens with blessed souls. So, souls, whether like this or like that, have heaven and hell in themselves while they're still in the body. Heaven is omnipresent, because God is in heaven. In the same way, hell is also present everywhere, because the devil is in hell and because (as the Book of Prayer teaches us) the whole world lies in evil. Not only is the devil in the world, but the world is also in the devil. Try to understand what heaven is. It is nothing other than the conversion of the human will to the love of God. Know, son, that when the very foundation of the soul offers itself to God, then it hides from itself and goes beyond all places that exist and can be imagined, to some unknown depth where only God manifests himself. And where only He acts and where there is only his will. Then the soul becomes nothing to itself and its own deeds and desires. God then dwells in that will which has renounced itself. And thereupon God works in it and has desires in place of it. In this case, when the body loses strength, the soul is in paradise. As the temple of the Holy Spirit. Like God's heaven in which he dwells. That is what is called the entry of the will into paradise, and that is how it happens."

Even though I memorized every word, I didn't understand a thing he said. I had to ask for additional explanation, to which I got an even more incomprehensible answer. Which does not lessen its value. Did not the Great Meister Eckhart say, "A God whom I could understand I wouldn't be able to worship." Good advice should be followed, and not understood.

"The godlike soul," Böhme went on, "is in Jesus' hand, that is, in heaven. But the ungodly soul is not willing to enter into the renunciation of its will in this life, nor to enter into God's will, but continues to wander about in its own wants and desires, in vanity and lies. And thus it turns to the will of the devil. Therefore, it accepts nothing but weakness, nothing but lies, pride, lust, envy, and anger. And to this it surrenders all its will and all its longing. That is the vanity of the will. And that vanity or empty shadow must similarly manifest itself in the soul."

I was disturbed by these words. Completely confused. I was a little remorseful that I had embarked on things beyond my means, instead of contenting myself with being an ordinary shoemaker, who would, admittedly, be stuck in hell, but who, at least while alive, would not be tormented by the knowledge that he would be going there. The teachings of Master Böhme are really full of contradictions, and if I had not personally been convinced of his honesty and—I can say this—holiness, I would have considered them to be a hoax. Because, in one place, Böhme says "renounce your will," in another, again, "transform your will into God's love". But how can I transform a will which I no longer have because I renounced it? Not a single word.

At that moment, I noticed that the blessed shoemaker was no longer walking but hovering some half a yard above the ground, carried by a gentle breeze.

"It is impossible for such a soul," he said, "to enter into God's peace. Because in it, God's wrath appears and acts. When such a soul is separated from the body, then eternal melancholy and desperation begin. Because only then does the soul realize that it has completely turned into vanity that eats away at itself, into destructive rage, into a self-torturing abomination. It is now disappointed with everything that brought it joy, it is blind, it is naked, wounded, and hungry and thirsty. Without even the slightest chance that it will ever be released or receive even one drop of the Water of Eternal Life. It feels that it is its own executioner and torturer. It is intimidated by its own ugly form, like the scariest worm, and would gladly run away from itself if it could, but cannot, being firmly bound by the bonds of the Dark Nature into which it plunged while in the body. Unaccustomed to immersing itself in God's mercy, obsessed with the idea of God as an angry and jealous God, the poor soul is frightened and ashamed to offer its will to God, by which it might be liberated."

After that day, Master Böhme never left the workshop again. Nor did he ever enter his home again. His purification was complete, and lady Katarina's tortures were no longer necessary. "Look, Schwenekpfeld," he told me, lying on the bare bench where he spent his final days, "we have to deliver thirty-seven more pairs of boots. You must make them by yourself, because I'm too weak to do it. When you finish the job, I will be able to die in peace." I tried to slow down my work in order to spend a little more time with my beloved master, but he did not permit me to dawdle. Böhme's death, however, was nowhere near those painful German partings with the soul, accompanied by howls, wailing, and general upset. Far from it. May God forgive me, it was actually a magnificent sight. His soul, long since immersed in God's will, calmly watched the burial of his body. About the time when I finished the twentieth pair of boots, the master's penis fell off. "Don't be surprised by that," he said, "the first to go are the limbs of sin." Then, in a miraculous way, he who had not produced a stool for the last few years, expelled the remains of his innards and intestines. In the end, he became completely transparent, and he did not speak any longer. The shoemaker and chosen servant of God, Jakob Böhme, gave up the ghost at the very moment when I finished the last pair of boots. I went to inform lady Katarina and to make funeral arrangements. But when we returned to the workshop, instead of the master's body on the bench, we found only a handful of golden dust resembling pollen. Or actually: resembling the powder that covers a butterfly's wings.

CRISIS AND AGONY

I sink in deep mire, where there is no standing:
I am come into deep waters, where the floods overflow me.

Psalms 69:2

1912. A series of bloody Balkan wars. The Western press (England again in the lead) writes with disgust about "the savagery, barbarity, and cruelty of the warring armies." For the geopolitics of parkinsonism, however, those wars are of inestimable significance, because they pave the way to Atatürk's reforms. "This isn't war at all," Parkinson announces at a soirée, "this is just the first battle of a great war in which the savagery, barbarianism, and cruelty of the 'civilized' world comes to the surface. In medical terms, the Balkan war is the contamination phase. The incubation phase is next. After that, my disease will purify this sinful world."

1912. A close friend of Demyan Lavrentyevich, Count Vronsky, goes to an audience with the Tsar. On his knees, he entreats the Tsar to throw the month of October out of the calendar for a period of twenty years.

Count Vronsky is removed to an insane asylum in an emergency procedure.

Parkinson's disease enters the Medical Encyclopedia.

A pioneer of Russian aeronautics, V. D. Bezdetnyi, circles above

Moscow in a bright red biplane and tosses out tracts with the continuation of the *Tractatus antiheliocentricus* printed on an underground press.

TRACTATUS ANTIHELIOCENTRICUS

PART TWO

The modern connection between politics and history is fundamentally wrong because the meaning of politics, that is, in its original meaning, urbanism, is the opposition to history.[9] One of the strategic functions of the city walls is to stop history. Because, when history enters the city, it leads to robbery, demolition, desecration, and killing. That's the way it was, and that's how it will go on. Striving to keep historical events as far away from the city center as possible, the policy of city walls maintains a necessary tension and ensures the authenticity of the events. Raw historical power is exhausted in long sieges. Nomads who once conquered the city and settled in it were cultivated very quickly; the next generation defended the walls under which new nomads encamped. It was a closed system in which events were recycled without creating the mental pollution characteristic of our times.

***

The absence of walls, finally, marks the end of the separation of cultural order and barbarism, and the beginning of a permanent state

9. The Chinese went one step further. With the Great Wall, they defined the entire territory of their country. The wall was simultaneously a barrier to the invasion of barbarians, and a dam which stopped the outflow of traditional values.

of siege in which those who attack and defend the city are mixed in a social solution equated with national affiliation that erases qualitative differences between individuals. This new state of social confusion is called democracy, the republic, or the nation-state.

***

The politicization of space and the expansion of political power have made modern states into quite vulnerable systems for the simple reason that control of the entire territory is physically impossible. Modern governance is largely unrealistic, since it is not exercised by hierarchically giving the authority of a specific person to another specific person for a specific purpose, but those powers are obtained from a depersonalized "state" by a certain number of persons to simulate the omnipresence of the state. That's how the bureaucratic apparatus comes about. In practice, no one is ever—not even during massive war operations—concerned with the entire territory. We are always in a specific space, that is, in the place where we are, including the horizon around it. But it is precisely this real space that is left at the mercy of the elements of chance, because the concern of state agencies is focused on the whole of a virtual territory that does not exist anywhere except on geographical maps.

***

Searching for the beginnings of the geometrization and politicization of space, we go back to the Renaissance. The generally accepted opinion, more precisely dogma, claims that the Renaissance was a period of exceptional importance for world history. That it was a brilliant period of prosperity after the long "dark" medieval period.

However, in contrast to that Manichaean, illuminist historical methodology, which operates on the concepts of light-dark, we must set the view that, in an integral sense, all periods of history are equally important, and that the "progressiveness" of the Renaissance is relevant only in the optics of secularized modern historicism whose foundations were laid and which were largely shaped precisely in the age of the Renaissance.

The key change that the Renaissance introduced was the altering of projection and perception. The Christian world is vertically oriented. Its goals are placed high above the plane of the empire,[10] and all its energy is directed toward a destination that lies beyond space and time. Consequently, all of medieval society was organized vertically, in the form of a class pyramid tightly interconnected by a precise system of subordination that offered everyone—regardless of class—the possibility of the highest achievements in the existing hierarchy of values. Everyone could be saved, and everyone could become a holy man. According to the then valid criteria, those were the highest values; material wealth and political power did not make it easier but more difficult to achieve the goal of earthly existence. By the pure logic of things, a society organized in that way was one of limited horizontal mobility, in which most people spent their whole lives in one place, within the boundaries of the specific space in which they were born. This resulted in a high degree of social and territorial stability. War was limited both in spatial terms and in the number of those who participated in it or were affected by it. The process of dismantling the physical and

10. It would remain that way later as well, when religiosity declined and was exchanged with ideological projections. Just because ideologies operate with this-worldly things, it does not mean that their goals are not metaphysical.

customary obstacles that prevent the masses from "gaining power" was later called a rebirth, although it "actually meant the death of many things." The spirit of trade, whatever forms it has taken on in history, is always nomadic and always finds ways to break through the limitations that cultivation establishes in order to sublimate personal and social energies. The much-vaunted increase and acceleration of the circulation of capital and people during the Renaissance resulted in a purely quantitative population growth, exchange of goods, and the introduction of certain technical innovations related to them, but at the same time, it led to worsening hygienic conditions and terrible plague epidemics, things that were unknown in the middle ages, although they were later attributed to it in the general falsification of history, which also began at that time. We will notice that the alleged superiority of that age in relation to the previous one is derived from the numerical superiority of statistical data; this tendency of quantification and the disregard for quality in time became a phenomenon to which, in assessing reality, absolute trust was given, although in all that science the only exact data were those obtained by counting corpses.

***

The Renaissance introduced nothing authentic. All innovations from that period were either long known in other civilizations or arose as a consequence of a great necromancer séance in which the spirit of late antiquity was invoked, or they were a reduplication of already existing processes and phenomena. The very fact that a dead civilization, more precisely the period of its decline, was taken as the ideal of the "rebirth," raises doubts about the functionality of the attempt to restore it within a culture established on a completely different basis. In this light, the Renaissance was a regression, because the artificial application of exhausted models cannot be called anything else than the invocation of death. The hidden meaning of that regression is the indulgence of inertia and the desire to abandon the monotheistic vertical order in favor of the horizontal, polytheistic-animistic one, which does not place high demands on man. The expansion of horizons and fields of action in the domain of the phenomenal meant the restriction of human presence symbolically or on the metaphysical plane: descent from the medial branches of the tree of life to the dried trunk of the tree of history. Giving up the connection with the higher forms of existence produces what is traditionally called "reassembling eggs," that is, redirecting all energies and potentials to the material and biological space of existence, which over time led to limiting human will and perception to a closed system in which, further, deprived of contact with the hierarchical flows of energies, all the hierarchical relations on which civilization rests are left to decay.

***

1914. The fighting detachment of the Belgrade Lodge Black Hand kills Archduke Franz Ferdinand and his wife Sofia in Sarajevo. Parkinsonism experiences its brightest moments. As if the ideology of Demyan Lavrentyevich has become the fate of the world. This can clearly be seen in the films of the event. After the first, unsuccessful assassination attempt, the Archduke—instead of leaving Sarajevo, which is logical, and what he himself wants—reluctantly continues his visit, surrenders to fate, and is killed. The Serbian government rejects the Ultimatum of the Austro-Hungarian government, due to demands that are unacceptable for a sovereign country. The Great War is unavoidable.

1917. War operations unwind in the best possible order: all warring parties are suffering terrible losses, famine and epidemics are ravaging battlefields and cities, the world is on the verge of the saving knowledge that it has contracted a serious disease. However, the fortunes of war suddenly turn against parkinsonism. In Russia, the October Revolution breaks out, led by Vladimir Ilyich Lenin. Things quickly go downhill. The success of the revolution causes a worldwide epidemic of the most superficial optimism, and a few more sporadic revolutions. It now seems to the masses that sacrifices make sense, that it is enough to overthrow emperors, kings, and old orders to make the world a place of happiness.
Tsar Nikolai orders Count Vronsky to be taken out of the insane asylum in order to entrust him with command of the armed forces. "Your highness," Vronsky tells the Tsar, "I'm afraid it's too late now." Demyan Lavrentyevich Parkinson withdraws deep into the underground.

1917. Lenin issues an order to confiscate and destroy all the writings of Demyan Lavrentyevich. Fani Kaplan wounds Lenin in an assassination attempt.

1924. Vladimir Ilyich Lenin dies.
Joseph Vissarionovich Jughashvili orders that the corpse of the revolution's leader be embalmed and displayed in a transparent coffin.

***

1936. Hitler outlaws Parkinson's disease. The ill, including patients with profane parkinsonism, along with a number of doctors and pharmacists, end up in a concentration camp. Translations of Parkinson's books are burned in bonfires along with books by Jewish authors and decadents.

1937. Joseph Vissarionovich Stalin, whose Parkinsonism has long since mutated into the power-loving Parkinsonism B, receives allegedly reliable information that Demyan Lavrentyevich Parkinson has changed his appearance and identity, and has infiltrated the very top of the Soviet leadership. In the years to come, Stalin will carry out a thorough purge of the military, state, and party apparatus. It is not certain whether it is paranoia, an unclean conscience or a sixth sense, or all that together, his associates testify that only Joseph Vissarionovich feels (or intuits) Parkinson's presence and actions. He orders the arrest of as many people as possible in the hope that Demyan Lavrentyevich is among them.

1938. A certain shoemaker from Novosibirsk, Nikolai Nikolayevich Kuznetsov, is arrested and taken to a camp on the Kolyma. Sixty years later, it will be established that this was the last identity of Demyan Lavrentyevich.

1938. Parkinson's disease is removed from the *Medical Encyclopedia.*

1947. Demyan Lavrentyevich Parkinson, alias N. N. Kuznetsov, dies on the Kolyma, never revealing his real identity.

1948. An obscure Russian language magazine, *The Afterlife,* which comes out in Paris, publishes the statement of Pavel Florensky in its September edition.

Pavel Aleksandrovich Florensky

Artistic prose and secular philosophy are certainly not subjects of much interest to me. Still, I will briefly (I don't have much time), meddle in the discussion of Parkinson's disease (of diseases in general), which I quite accidentally, it's not important how, heard about here in the camp for the unreformable in Solovki. So, I will spend my time the best possible way, while waiting for the arrival of NKVD lieutenant Vasilyev, who will fire a bullet into the back of my head. There may be some use of my speaking up. If a good soul accidentally reads this, which I doubt, please inform my wife Ana Mikhailovna that a letter arrived from Leningrad this morning stating: "Florensky, Pavel Aleksandrovich is to be shot." Underneath: "Secretary of the Troika: Lt. G.B. Sorokin, head of the Third Department of the NKVD."

It is better for her to find out about my death immediately than to rely on the disinformation of the General Administration of the camp, which for some reason delays such announcements for several years. The most important moment in the life of every Christian is death. My friends and relatives should know that I am dead.

However, we should not cultivate bad feelings towards Professor Gudilyanov, who, although we have never met, accused me of membership in a secret fascist organization, the Nationalist Center for Russian Renewal, which does not exist at all. Nor should we hate the signatory of my death sentence, Lieutenant Sorokin, because he is only the executor of God's will. A mere instrument of Sagaciousness. Yes, Sagaciousness. We live in a time of extreme alienation and apostasy, in which Providence must also act externally. Using all available means. Even the NKVD. Who among us today, weakened as we are, would voluntarily undergo a stoning? Who would dare to enter the arena among the wild beasts? But we must save ourselves. Well, if there is no steadfast faith and inner determination, it is right for others to stone us and throw us among the beasts. Furthermore, it is utterly wrong to view the Soviet state with all its repressive apparatus as a political system; it must be understood as a disease. I will not exaggerate if I say that the foundations of this "communist monster," as it is called in the West, were laid by a colorful, highly respected society of philosophers, writers and scientists; people of vision; prisoners of liberty in a secular sense; philanthropists dedicated to "improving the living conditions of the broadest strata"; coryphes of hygiene and prophylaxis; preachers of vaccination. Few people during the hundred-year campaign have wondered: what's the good of that? All those things benefit exclusively the body, and harm the soul. Besides the fact that they are absolutely impossible to carry out. All of it as a theory originates in the West. But only Russia has the strength to undertake the execution of the impossible. And for that courage it is rewarded with the terrible but cleansing disease of Bolshevism. It is Bolshevism that is turning Russia from a hotbed of indulgence, fornication, and debauchery, into the Sinai Desert, into an endless space of forced asceticism. Why then be judgmental of Sorokin and Vasilyev? They should receive our blessings. Anyway, the unhappy fellows will end up in the fires of hell. Because, unlike the rules of the earth, the one who performs the work of Providence is not released from responsibility.

Mother Russia should therefore be seen as a sanatorium. The NKVD, KGB, Gulag, Lubyanka and a network of smaller prisons—as departments of the divine polyclinic. And we should love the persecutors because they push us on a narrow path that we would not otherwise take. The commandment to love our enemies does not mean that they deserve it. Far from it. They are degenerates. But what good is it if we love only our neighbors? Even the Sorokins love those closest to them. I once wrote that a person without love is broken into many fragmentary psychological particles and elements. Love is a mysterious kind of glue. If that glue, however, sticks only paper and wood together, and not glass and iron, then it is the glue of doom, not the glue of ascension. We must love our enemies because—we have to be certain of this—we are no better than they are. We were just luckier.

Demyan Lavrentyevich Parkinson, whom I once, it seems to me, met at the gate of the Smolny convent, is quite right when he calls for people to voluntarily get sick. So to say—to rush into illness. To complete a commitment to being ill. Because it is our faith, faith in paradox. The only way for us to get healthy is indeed for us to be sick. And to be proud of our disease, just like St. Paul who says, *Most gladly therefore will I rather glory in my infirmities.* And also, *my strength is made perfect in weakness.* I would have more to say, of course, but now footsteps can be heard in the hallway. That's Lieutenant Sorokin coming to execute me. I should kneel (interesting: it's the same position for praying and for being executed) and pray that some good soul will read these lines and send a message to my wife, Ana Mihailovna: This morning from Leningrad a message arrived stating, "Florensky, Pavel Aleksandrovich is to be shot."

1949. Parkinson's disease re-listed in the *Medical Encyclopedia,* now with altered symptoms and clinical picture.

1949. A self-published edition of the *Tractatus antiheliocentricus* appears in Leningrad on cigarette paper, containing only one sentence:

"There is a legend according to which the Great Wall of China is in fact a huge ideogram which in translation means, 'You have reached my base. You shall go no further! Now go away, you scum!'"

1949. In its July edition, the *Afterlife* magazine publishes a story which the ghost of a Turkish officer killed in the First Balkan War told to Zahgayevsky, the necromancer.

Mehmet Ali Murtadoğlu

A TALE ABOUT PARKINSON

[. . .] The Cossacks on the borders of the Empire were a tactical illusion. A mere distraction. It was not the Russian masses, but one single Russian who drove the Ottoman Empire to its knees. It was the medical officer Demyan Lavrentyevich Parkinson. A doctor who turned into his own disease, and then infected the Colossus on the Bosporus with it. The writings of those who never had the privilege of stepping into the Ottoman Empire (let alone living there) now assure us that the collapse of the empire was conditioned by some "growing contradictions," some "aspiration of small peoples for liberation." Notorious nonsense. Empires are created and based on these contradictions and aspirations. And they disappear, die, and get lost in history due to common diseases, plague, Spanish fever, cholera, just like people.

Because empires are not states, but living beings.

Many epidemics have swept through the Ottoman Empire over the centuries. Some were even caused on purpose. Epidemics were, in fact, the source of its strength. Only as such, cleansed of the weak, the corrupt and the cowards (who are the only ones susceptible to infections), could the Empire spread like a plague across the expanses of Europe and Asia. It also suffered from Parkinson's ridiculous disease. Which isn't even lethal.

Joining the Sultan's army, Parkinson first infected the military. Somewhat earlier, under cowardly pressures, the army was modernized by introducing medical units. This concession weakened the Empire's immunity. As an experienced officer, I claim: for real armies, medical units are not only unnecessary but also harmful. First of all, they are not combat formations. Those are groups of parasites, paramedics, and doctors who, contrary to the logic of war—to kill as many soldiers on all warring sides as possible—do their best to cure and revive them as best they can. Thus, they make the world more and more sick. The true purpose of warfare is not to achieve political goals by military means, as von Clausewitz sees it (it is secondary) but *prophylaxis*: cleansing national herds of the weak, the sick, and the fearful. The best-ordered societies, which unfortunately no longer exist, owe their tenacity to epidemics and wars. In terms of strategy, medical units are an unnecessary ballast: they slow down combat operations, increase costs (transportation, food, medicine, medical supplies), and provide sad scenes in the field hospitals that weaken the morale of the fighters. In terms of strategy, things are even worse. A soldier who is killed is not worth a red cent. That is clear to everyone. But the wounded are worth even less, and they cost incomparably more. One paramedic, however, even if he has a rank, not only has no value, but should actually have to pay extra to the state because he exists at all.

Serious officers knew even then that the introduction of medical units would not work out. The more far-sighted foresaw with sadness the arrival of dismal times in which barracks would be turned into hospitals, and in which there would be only two classes of people in the world: doctors and patients. However, an Imperial *firman* was proclaimed. And the Imperial is not to be disobeyed. Although even an Imperial *firman* does not have the authority to introduce modernization before modernity. There were only a few doctors in Turkey at that time; they, and disease in general, were looked down upon. Military doctors even more so. That is why they started the recruitment of medical officers from the armies of Europe. A well-established practice at that time. Back then, officers were still officers. It was important to do battle. It did not matter on whose side. (In every war, only the weakest, dead, and maimed are losers, no matter who they belong to. The military class always wins.) In that context, Captain Parkinson also appeared from somewhere. With a perfect knowledge of Turkish. We concluded from his surname that he was English. Maybe a Scotsman. It never occurred to anyone to check into him. In those days, officers still had honor, and only weaklings and cowards dealt with background checks.

At first, Parkinson left a good impression on me. We got closer. I also introduced him to Mustafa Kemal. The First Balkan War was ongoing. The fortunes of war had turned their back on us. Serbs, Greeks, and Bulgarians were advancing on all fronts. For the first time in their existence, the sultan's glorious soldiers retreated. What was worse, they were reluctant to die. They hesitated to attack. They were taking cover. They were shooting without aiming. Ubiquitous field hospitals were spreading their devastating effects. Parkinson, too most probably, but I still didn't doubt him then. Officers, understandably, must preserve their presence of mind. We drink tea, smoke, and talk in the officer's dugouts in the trenches. That Parkinson knew how to talk. To spread his contagion with sweet and learned words. Mustafa Kemal was fascinated by the chatty doctor. I must admit, so was I. Until that morning when I woke up and saw that there had been a replacement during the night. There seemed to be no sign of Parkinson. In fact, Parkinson in the form of Mustafa Kemal. They were similar in stature and appearance, except that Parkinson had green eyes and Kemal, as befits a Turk, had dark eyes. Thanks to the magical powers of transformation, Parkinson had turned into Mustafa. But he didn't manage to change the color of his eyes. I did not miss that detail. "Don't be crazy, Mehmet!" he shouted at me when I openly told him that I had seen through the fraud. "Captain Parkinson was wounded in the arm last night while you were asleep drunk as a skunk. He tried to perform the amputation himself with his healthy hand. But it didn't work. Then a paramedic accepted the job and, inexperienced as he was, amputated his head instead of his arm. It's war! It happens. Now, to the trenches with you!"

I soon got a chance to get acquainted with all the misery of the military medical staff. Following the western fashion, in addition to ordinary doctors who amputated legs and bandaged wounds, from somewhere there were also doctors for mental illness. The regimental commander sent me to one for an examination. He glanced off-handedly at the referral. He tapped me beneath the knee with a tiny hammer. And he said I needed a vacation. Then he sent me on vacation: right to the most advanced position, where I probably died in a fight with bloodthirsty Serbs, giving my fellow soldiers an example of how to die for the Sultan. I don't know. I'm not really sure. Who could know in all that turmoil?

I know my story sounds crazy. I knew that even then, but my honor as an officer demanded that I expose the conspiracy. That's how it goes: at one point, the usual order of things is disturbed, someone sees it and—if he is truthful—he brings misery upon himself. Insanity does not exist. Everyone who is considered a lunatic must have seen something terrible once in their life. Something they cannot let go of. Something they have to talk about, regardless of the price they will pay. And I paid a high price. Provided that I got out alive, I ended up in Serbian captivity. Where, due to the similarity between the languages, the discussion often turned into

Bulgarian. Then into Greek, even though the languages are not similar. Meanwhile, the fake Kemal was somewhere in Anatolia. He was rapidly climbing the ladder of success, which, it is clear to sober minds, was the ladder to the collapse of the Ottoman Empire.

It wasn't long before you could meet real Turks only in those Serbian-Bulgarian-Greek prisons and prison camps where to varying degrees, they resisted becoming Christians, Serbs, Bulgarians, or Greeks.

1951. The periodical *La Nouvelle Revue Française* prints a story by Vladimir Nabokov.

Vladimir Nabokov

HOW DOSTOYEVSKY GAMBLED AWAY RUSSIA

At the time of my youth among Russian emigrants in Germany, there was a story circulating about how Dostoyevsky gambled away a fabulous amount of money in a Swiss casino in just three nights, which could have saved Russia from the Bolsheviks. Due to the semi-divine status that this writer (in my opinion unjustifiably) enjoys, the story was transmitted exclusively by word of mouth, usually in the dead of night. With a whisper at that. It is certainly the fruit of exile resentment, a somewhat understandable need to alleviate the cruelty of the past with imaginary alternatives and fictitious possibilities that give rise to an even more fictitious belief that things could have gone in a completely different direction. I think that it could not have happened. That Dostoyevsky may be charged with squandering (as we shall see) twice that much money, yes; but not for the downfall of tsarist Russia. The story, however, certainly deserves to be told again.

The plot of the story is set in the years of great disturbance between 1870 and 1900, the years of confusion in which the chronology (very dubious, after all) was subsequently and rather arbitrarily determined. It will never be known with certainty what precedes what, nor will the sequence of causes and effects ever be determined. It was a time of the flourishing obscure cults and mad ideologies, an age of general decadence and eerie ruination. Entirely in the Russian spirit, all that turmoil, however, is perceived as an ascent. As progress. As the beginning of a new era. More precisely, of new eras. Because all those schools of weird thinking and even weirder beliefs claim the exclusive right to own the truth and the future. My relationships with God are complicated, indirect; they take place very slowly through a multitude of protocols, mediators, and interpreters, so that I can be considered an atheist, although I am convinced that beyond all the "beyonds" God still exists, and that he is quite dissatisfied with the Russians and Russia. Especially dissatisfying to God is the very hateful tendency of the Russians towards exaggeration, gigantism, exaltation above all human measures. Even in my meager theology, there is a teaching that God is merciful or long-suffering. But the sin of the Russians is overwhelming. No one can stand it. Not even God. If he had endured it, he would not be God, but a double of someone from the constellation of imaginary imbeciles from a Dostoyevsky novel. Namely, the Russians are arrogantly interfering in God's work; they want to save the world on their own (or, in a more moderate version, at least the Slavic world), all the while sitting in Moscow and St. Petersburg taverns. All the while drinking countless glasses of moonshine.

God will cruelly show them that they do not even have enough strength to save themselves.

We will leave aside the wealth of literary material from that crazy age and focus on the story of dishonorable money that was supposed to serve to save the honor of such a Russia. Especially since I personally knew one of its key heroes: Demyan Lavrentyevich Parkinson. Although no one knew for sure who Parkinson was, what his education was, what his profession was, he was what we today call a *celebrity*. A regular guest of intellectual and literary salons, a tireless participant in endless and meaningless discussions, a favorite of the ladies, and a flirt (so-called free love was already in vogue). It was rumored, and he did not deny, that he had an affair with Lou Salomé, the later fatal love of Friedrich Nietzsche. That must have been true because there was a certain resemblance between Nietzsche and Parkinson. At least as far as the shape of their mustaches is concerned. But, despite the vagueness and ambiguity of Parkinson's personality and his affairs, he was an educated man, a polite and pleasant conversation partner. It was also rumored that he had an acute attack of some disease in his early youth; perhaps it was epilepsy, which would not be strange if we keep in mind the strong influence of Dostoyevsky, and thereby his epilepsy, on the family of Demyan Lavrentyevich. That attack allegedly had a decisive influence on his later development, which I had the opportunity to learn about firsthand, during a conversation with Parkinson, in St. Petersburg, in the café of the *Pribaljtijskaja Hotel.* Namely, he was famous for his bizarre theory, amalgam of mysticism, mysticism and twisted philosophy, according to which states of illness and health, together with countless intermediate states, are primarily a political, not a medical problem; it is a theory which, furthermore, teaches that there is essentially only one disease—life as such—and that the multitude of diseases in modern pathology is a mere consequence of the desacralization of that disease and its decline in industrialization.

A combination of somewhat strange circumstances had brought me to the hotel that afternoon (or morning, it was the season of white nights)—I can't resist writing that name in Cyrillic—*Прибальтискаја.* Demyan Lavrentyevich, who happened to be there, noticed me and invited me to have tea, which I gladly accepted, since the same set of circumstances made a certain lady completely inexplicably not be in room 412. I started the conversation with a courteous question, an inevitable one during white nights in St. Petersburg. "So, Demyan Lavrentyevich, how did you sleep?" And I got a bizarre answer. "It's been a few months since I slept." It didn't make sense to continue with politeness. I got straight to the point. "Tell me, Parkinson, something more about your theory, which is talked about a lot, but superficially in Moscow. If I understood correctly, you think that medicine, with the exception of surgery, orthopedics, and some traditional methods of treatment, is in fact a fraudulent science. I'm not a big fan of medicine myself. However, I would like to know more about it." "You see, Nabokov," said Demyan Lavrentyevich, "I am convinced that you yourself know quite well that at this time there is no science that is not fraudulent. And the thing is as such because the foundations of modern science are false. The notion of celestial mechanics—which our contemporaries are unreasonably proud of—this very notion, therefore, our elementary picture of the universe, is fundamentally wrong. It is possible to determine relatively precisely the date of the beginning of the falsification of everything and everyone. It is a fragment of time in which the geocentric model of the world was, so to speak, overnight, replaced by the heliocentric one . . ."

I couldn't help but ask, "Don't you think, Parkinson, that it doesn't matter at all to human affairs whether we think the Earth or the Sun is at the center of the universe?" "Of course it matters, Nabokov," said Demyan Lavrentyevich. "I will try to explain to you in the briefest possible way why it matters. I will use a slightly vulgarized comparison. You, for example, I happen to know, have a large apartment in the center of Moscow. That apartment determines your geographical and psychological position in Moscow, and from that position arises an attitude, a feeling, a certain security that is drastically different from the feelings, attitude and habitus of an Ivan Ivanovich who lives in a hovel somewhere on the outskirts of the city. Now that comparison should be applied to celestial mechanics. As long as it was thought that the center of the universe was the Earth, it actually was. I note that movement should be abstracted. Movement is relative. What is moving in relation to something else is not an exact fact, but a matter of consensus . . .

"And so what?" Parkinson exclaimed. "If the Earth is in the center of the world, then we, its inhabitants, take a central place and feel like you feel in your Moscow apartment. We feel comfortable. We're safe. God is close. At our fingertips, as they say. Well, then troublemakers enter the historical scene, absolutizing the relativity of their own perceptions and starting to set things upside down. (It is a real miracle, I thought, that the creator of heliocentrism is not Russian.) They say: The Sun is in the center. And everyone takes their word for it. What happens next? Rare documents from that time report terrible epidemics of dizziness that ravaged Europe when it was rumored that the Earth was turning. They talk about the suicides of disappointed believers. It is important to mention that we have become accustomed to this nausea over the centuries. Or we attribute it to other causes. It does not matter. Even if we don't feel it, we are suffering from dizziness. From the 'Copernican Revolution' onwards, humanity feels like that Ivan Ivanovich from the Moscow suburbs. It's becoming provincial. It's becoming self-centered. Embittered. Aggressive. If the Earth is not in the center, then nothing is in the center."

"It's an interesting theory, Demyan Lavrentyevich, but I don't see a connection between the Copernican Revolution and medicine." Parkinson looked at me a little scornfully. "There is a connection, Nabokov. But history, a science even more charlatan than medicine, keeps silent about many things. It is almost unknown, for example, that medicine as a science did not exist at all before the 'Copernican Revolution.' There were doctors, but medicine did not exist. Like most of the diseases that are ravaging the world today. At that time, we had only a few diseases, diseases that were healing at the same time. Those were leprosy, plague, cholera, drought, dropsy, and gout. End of the list. People accepted these diseases as a means of purification, as penances, and no reasonable person tried to cure them or themselves. Everything changed, almost overnight, by accepting the heliocentric model of the universe. Instead of caring for the immortal soul, people begin to worry about health—a thing, therefore, obviously, lost in advance." Though Scots or Irishmen by ancestry, the Parkinsons had gradually become Russians after only three generations. Parkinson's theory, for example, contains all the few virtues and all the many flaws of Russian thought. This view of things looks more tragic and deeper than the West, but that depth lacks breadth. In the process of the articulation of the problem, its Russification occurs, which is in itself wrong because the problems are universal. That, however, is not all. In parallel with the Russification of religious and philosophical insights goes their Messianization. No matter how valuable the thing he learned, the Russian immediately ruins it with the desire to improve it and put it in the service of saving the world. Russia's exaggeration in noble causes always ends in pride, as an infernal need to change the structure of the world and matter, and finally, as a barely concealed intention to turn the universe into Russia.

If it's not good for theology and philosophy, it's great for literature. (Russian intellectuals generally behave like literary heroes. Perhaps the project of Parkinson senior—turning Russia into one huge novel—wasn't absolutely utopian, perhaps it could even have succeeded.) So, I continued the discussion. "Well, all right, Demyan Lavrentyevich, what can be done? Can any of that be changed? Is there any sense in changing anything at all?" There was still a lot of Scottish left in Parkinson. If he had been a pure-blooded Russian, upon hearing my question he would undoubtedly have jumped up, downed two hundred grams of vodka, blushed, and started screaming; as it was, Parkinson took a sip of tea and said measuredly:

"Perhaps something could be done. And I am going to try to do something. However, the chances of people turning away from health care in favor of spiritual care are not too high in the world as it is at the moment. Signs of the times! Signs of the times, Nabokov. Just look at the flourishing of spas and thermal baths. Look at all those educated and well-mannered people rolling around the muddy puddles like pigs and everything will be clear to you. And even worse things are happening. If there are people with certain mild disorders in the spas, that is somewhat justified, although it is still meaningless. But how to explain the appearance of completely healthy people who travel hundreds of kilometers to lie on the beach? That so-called tourism will surely give birth to something much, much worse." From this distance, I'm almost certain that Parkinson had in mind the later appearances of Fascism and Nazism. And he was right. Tourism is indeed unarmed Nazism.) "A certain success," Parkinson continued, "might be achieved not by spiritualization but by the incomparably more acceptable politicization of disease in our time . . ." I interrupted him again. "Demyan Lavrentyevich, you didn't tell me anything about your infamous disease." Parkinson didn't seem to hear the question. The Russian had overpowered the Scotsman. "The disease, therefore, should be turned into an ideology, into a political movement. If this is not done, Nabokov, the rise of ideologies of false health awaits us, which will make the disease incurable. You ask me about the disease. And I ask you: do you have the strength to hear the truth about the disease?" "Yes!" I said with surprising decisiveness. "Perhaps I don't have the strength to be ill. But I am strong enough to hear the truth."

"Then hear me well. There is only one disease. But it manifests itself differently in each person. It is the disease of the Fall. You certainly know the story of the Fall, even though you are probably an atheist. I'm religious, but I still like to simplify things. I would rather call the Fall an interruption. The energies of the spiritual world had not yet completely permeated the nothingness of matter in Adam when the affair with the Tree of the Knowledge of Good and Evil took place, the interpretation of which is better not to indulge in. It is the cause of our later inherited diseases. Then we come to 'health.' In order not to despair—and there are good reasons to do so, believe me—God conceals our true condition from ourselves; through gracious energies, He gives us a sense of health so that we have the strength to face our illness. Unfortunately, we understand this temporary gift as personal property, even as an inalienable right. I have had the rare fortune that this 'health' has been temporarily taken away from me several times in order to be convinced experientially of the nausea, horror, and emptiness of a fallen life. And for practical reasons, I called it 'Parkinson's disease.' Have you ever had a terrible hangover, Nabokov? Several times, you say. Well, the state of the most terrible hangover is somewhat similar to an acute attack of parkinsonism."

"Well, Demyan Lavrentyevich," I said somewhat ironically, "we Russians, a people prone to alcohol and consequently severe hangovers, should be the ideal milieu for the execution of your political project."

Parkinson waved his hand in resignation. "It won't happen! We

Russians ruin everything. We cannot be healthy or sick. The primitive concept of sick leave in Russia, the simple focus on the physical and physiological aspects of the disease, further aggravate the situation. Sick-leave in our country usually turns into gloomy and lethargic laziness. Into complete passivity. Remember, Nabokov, being sick is a very serious business."

Leaving the *Pribaljtijskaja Hotel,* I was not entirely certain whether Parkinson was crazy or just another of the enthusiasts of the time who blindly believed in their own fantastic theories. Sometime later, in Moscow, at a dinner with Countess V., I told Nikolai Berdyaev some details from the conversation with Parkinson, despite the fact that, if the chronology is to be believed, the two of us would meet a few years later. Berdyaev took Parkinson much more seriously than I did. (Just as much as he was a more serious man anyway.) "What can I tell you, Nabokov?" said the great thinker. "Parkinson is half right. His research of disease is profound, and often accurate. However, his intention to make a political movement out of it is wrong. You ask me if he is crazy or not? Who knows? In any case, even if he is crazy, his madness should not be confused with his theories. There is some truth here. Listen to this. According to Parkinson, the first man to suffer from Parkinson's disease, the first sick man in human history in general, was righteous Job. Before him, diseases did not exist; people were dying of old age, tired of life. Job's disease cost him a lot, and was the prototype of all future diseases. But at the same time, it was also instruction for healing. Think about it! Having fallen sick, Job did nothing. He accepts illness and unspeakable suffering as an expression of God's will. As a path of purification that only the righteous deserve. He knows that the complete healing of fallen nature is preceded by absolute disease. There are no healthy organs in his body. The Old Testament book only mentions the visible changes to his skin. For the sake of the economy of salvation. Because there are few who were able to read the complete list without being arrogant themselves. But mystical writings intended for the spiritually stronger, describe in detail the terrible inflammations, tumors, and internal bleeding. Job, however, spells out a sentence that much later St. Paul (also a very sick man) will write in one of his epistles: "Until life devours death." He learns in suffering that disease does not destroy health, but disease; just as death does not destroy life, but itself. The lesson of righteous Job is this: the only cure is patience. Patience gives birth to hope. Hope gives birth to love. And love brings healing. There is no place for any kind of doctors or drugs."

Berdyaev fell silent for a few moments, then said:

"According to Parkinson, Alexander the Great also suffered from parkinsonism. Although history remembers him as a conqueror, this great Greek is in fact a mystic. Born in the Macedonian mountains, raised in the spirit of simplicity and moderation, he realizes that abundance, luxury, and debauchery are leading the Hellenic world to certain doom. It is not worth telling such people about voluntary suffering. That is why Alexander approaches surgical treatment, cutting off heads, legs, and arms, and then infects Helena, cleansed in blood baths, with life-saving Parkinson's disease, from which he himself suffers. The Greeks would never have accepted Christianity if Alexander had not taught them to be sick. However, he does not limit himself to his homeland. He wanted to make the disease universal. He didn't go to India to conquer territory, but rather to spread the disease. If you ask me, that's completely correct."

Many years have passed since meeting Demyan Lavrentyevich in St. Petersburg—but certainly not as many as the chronology full of inaccuracies and exaggerations claims—and I long ago lost (without even reading it) a small pamphlet entitled *Parkinson's Disease Through the Centuries,* which Parkinson gave me in the hope of preserving it or even writing about it one day when the story reaches me about how Fyodor Mikhailovich[11] gambled away the money intended for the liberation of Russia. Among the many fanatical fans of Fyodor Mikhailovich, the story goes, Parkinson's father, Lavrentiy Akakyevich, stood out with his fanaticism. A surveyor by education, Lavrentiy Akakyevich led a movement for years, or rather a sect of opponents of replacing traditional decimal units. Since this replacement is now a *fait accompli,* with all the consequences Parkinson senior pointed out in vain, we will return to the field of literature, where versts, furlongs, and miles are still legitimately in use. According to the story, poor Lavrentiy Akakyevich had one fixed idea: he dreamed that one day Dostoyevsky would mention him in the most remote corner of a novel. Dostoyevsky, by the way, often went to the Parkinsons' estate, which over time had become an impossible mixture of secret society, mystical brotherhood, prostitution, and gambling. Unlike his son, Lavrentiy Akakyevich never wrote anything. He wanted to be written about. But despite the absence of documents, we can reconstruct his

---

11. Demyan Lavrentyevich, as opposed to his father, did not have a high opinion of Dostoyevsky. He was actually the first one to rebel against the autocratic position which Fyodor Mikhailovich took up (and still holds) in Russian literature, which led me to later re-read and re-evaluate his works. Interestingly, Parkinson also thought that Dostoyevsky's notorious epilepsy was a simulation that the writer resorted to for two reasons: to arouse pity in his creditors and to strengthen the myth of his genius with that non-existent disease, even calling it "sacred." Parkinson interpreted his occasional and undeniable attacks and fainting spells as nervous exhaustion and long-lasting sleep deprivation because of gambling.

doctrine. He believes that it is possible to be redeemed through sin, by repeating, accumulating, multiplying sins, until the moment when sins are redeemed by absolute repentance. Complete metanoia. His summer house becomes a meeting place for the greats of fornication, debauchery, and corruption. Parkinson the elder is a patriot; he thinks it's so much better for Russia that way. If those debauchers are there, in one place, then their influence is localized in the already corrupt environment. If they are in Mitrofanovsk, then they cannot be in Moscow.

The problem is that those so-called gentlemen can easily be in Mitrofanovsk, Moscow, and the Crimea.

That's the kind of people they are. Among them is Dostoyevsky, who, as we said, often visits the Parkinsons. Supposedly, to collect material for the book *Notes from Underground,* which—everyone knows that except Lavrentiy Akakyevich—had long since been written. He actually comes to indulge his passion: gambling. Why does a famous writer like Fyodor Mikhailovich—someone will ask, and he must have wondered—not go to European casinos? Our writer knows the answer. And I will answer the uninformed: Fyodor Mikhailovich has no money.

Unlike Lavrentiy Akakyevich, who has it in abundance. And who is a generous man. He richly rewards the great writer every time. However, no one can have as much money as Dostoyevsky is able to devour. Lavrentiy Akakyevich is not bothered by those losses, he still has a lot of money; he is only sorry that Fyodor Mikhailovich's gambling table is more important than his writing. From time to time, he hints at it, he urges him on politely. And then we witness the terrible attacks of the writer's pseudo-epilepsy. "Write, you say!" roars Fyodor Mikhailovich, slowly coming to his senses. "Yes, write, but—how? I'm a realist writer, and here, in

Russia, there is no reality. I will be remembered as the father of the psychological novel, and where, I ask you, is the psychology? There is none! There is no reality, no psychology. Half of Russia indulges in morbid fantasies; the other half eats, drinks, and sleeps. Not a protagonist to be found! No man who would do something out of conviction, for a higher goal, and so on. Provide me with a topic, Lavrentiy Akakyevich, and I will get down to work. And maybe mention you somewhere in the novel, as a servant in a tavern, or as a police officer. There you have it!"

Lavrentiy Akakyevich made a fateful decision. Fyodor Mikhailovich was right. Fyodor Mikhailovich was always right. There is really no reality or psychology in Russia. But there are corrupt journalists. The servant harnessed the horses and Parkinson hurried off to Moscow, rushing across the snow-covered steppes and icy woods where—we see it in the magnifying glass—orphan boys and girls shiver by low fires to fit the whole scene into the sweet poetics of the time. The hack Samson Leonidich, a journalist from the *Moscow News*, has already received a telegram and is waiting patiently. "I need it, Samson Leonidich," Parkinson tells him, "I need a real, powerful, impressive event. Something unusual, to say the least. I'll pay handsomely. So, some sort of cruel murder. But not just any kind. The murder must be committed with higher motives." "Your excellence, Lavrentiy Akakyevich," said Samson Leonidich humbly, "there are no more such murders." "Then make one up!" Parkinson insisted. "For example, a failed student, disappointed in the human race, kills, say, a useless member of society. An old woman usurer. No one has to get killed. Make it up! Write a feuilleton. I will pay well, Samson Leonidich."

The deal is done. Akakyevich returns to Mitrofanovsk; the troika hurtles past that grove with the frozen orphans. In the troika, a bundle of the *Moscow News* that Parkinson puts by the bed of Fyodor Mikhailovich that same evening. The rest is the history of literature. If it weren't for Dostoyevsky's gambling obsession, that history could have moved in a completely different direction. Because Lavrentiy Akakyevich, under the influence of his son's theories, frightened by horrible visions—some say by delirium hallucinations—of the imminent collapse of Russia, was convinced that only a revolution in literature could prevent a revolution in the country. Lavrentiy Akakyevich advocates absolute realism, politically certainly useless, but interesting as a contribution to the history of Russian deviations.

Lavrentiy Akakyevich's revolutionary idea is basically simple: instead of novels being created and existing within the state, the state should be organized as literary material and formed into a novel. The execution of that idea, Parkinson is aware of that, is an incomparably more complex job. But not an impossible one. Russia has many capable writers. The problem is their love of originality, the fairground variety of ideas and themes. If these talents were united under the leadership of the Supreme Novelist (Dostoyevsky, of course), their creative energy would not be wasted, and the project could begin. Where the tsar is only a literary figure, even the central one, there is no room for arbitrariness. Not to mention the arbitrariness of subordinate officials. Writing (and in such a Russia all literate people would write) implies a high degree of concentration, concentration, in turn, ennobles, and nobility, ultimately, brings peace . . .

Lavrentiy Akakyevich wastes not a moment. He writes to Dostoyevsky. Invites him to get to work. The letter, by some miracle, has been preserved in its entirety.

Most Respected Fyodor Mikhailovich,

Batyushka,

You know of my long-held desire that you mention me in one of your future novels. On the other hand, I know of your principle that you use only fictional personalities in your prose. I also have understanding for that. If you give in only once, if you introduce a specific man or, far from it, a woman into your plots, that would be the beginning of the process of the degradation of realistic prose and its transformation into reality. And that is what we want to avoid at all costs. Unfortunately, I don't have a literary gift, but sometimes I have visions . . . Perhaps it is better to say: thanks to excessive alcohol use and the consequent disorder of the senses, from time to time I become an observer of certain performances, which I believe will begin to happen in the future. My son, Demyan Lavrentyevich, thinks that I am ill, but that those visions are credible. He goes a step further and claims that I deserve these visions precisely thanks to my illness. According to him, health is blindness, self-satisfaction, a state of infernal egoism that prevents us from seeing things as they are. And I believe him. Because the essence of the visions that I am witnessing concerns the historical crossroads where Russia is. And Mother Russia is not even aware of that. We are, Fyodor Mikhailovich, facing a fateful choice: either a sick individual and a healthy society; or a healthy individual and a sick community. There is no third option. And the other one, a state of cruel and evil athletes, is not a path but a roadless wilderness. Because, care for personal health, keeping organisms in good condition, especially when they become mass phenomena, weakens social cohesion and leads to absolute immorality.

The state is too serious a matter to be left at the mercy of lawyers and philosophers. And it is precisely these gentlemen who feel most invited to meddle in state affairs. The abstractness and speculation of these professions, in fact, their superficiality, are the cause of a growing decadence. In philosophical systems and codes, things seem to be in place, but the streams of real life flow in the opposite direction. Philosophers and jurists start from the incorrect premise that communities are composed of mentally and physically healthy people, and that in human communities mental and physical diseases are a disorder of the system, a step backwards, an anomaly. This is a dangerous misconception. Disease is a system, health an illusion. God's grace, a kind of heavenly anesthesia, takes into account the weakness of our nature and conceals disease until we reach maturity and attain the ability to perceive its healing properties. But today, fewer and fewer are those able to cope with their illnesses. It is almost impossible to find a patient who does not gasp, who does not ask the idiotic question "why is this happening to me?"; to make matters worse, even high-ranking officers go to the doctor and undergo humiliating examinations . . .

All this is a consequence of the modern contempt for war. Our intellectuals, brought up in the West, instead of war, propagate soap as a prophylactic. Soap, however, is powerless to cope with our pain. At best, it makes us clean, fragrant, which only makes the disease worse. Soap is useless. As you wrote with inspiration in the article "Does Spilled Blood Save": "On the contrary, not war but peace, long-lasting peace, will make a man a cruel beast. Long-lasting peace always cultivates triviality, cowardice and crude, fat egoism. And, most importantly, mental blockage. During a long peacetime, only the exploiters of the people are fattened."

The more cultured a nation is, the more it goes to war. In war, especially if it is motivated by some elevated idea, we all become instruments of the vector of higher powers; we all, so to speak, fit into the intentions of Providence. In peacetime, on the other hand, we all care exclusively for our health and personal gain, which leads to a degree of chaos that is increasingly difficult to control and that will inevitably end in disaster.

Fyodor Mikhailovich, Batyushka, if something is not done, Satan will soon take over the Kremlin.

My son, Demyan Lavrentyevich, is committed to politicizing our original, ancestral disease, to turning it into a political program. Even more so, into an idea. (Attached to the letter is his pamphlet "The Political Philosophy of Parkinson's Disease.") The essence of his doctrine is the necessity of a holy war of the sick against the imperialism of the healthy. You know very well how in Russia, probably also in other places, the sick are looked down upon. They are second-class citizens here. The untouchables. Just remember how they dress them in miserable rags and faded smocks in order to humiliate them to the end. How they are forced to lie in bed all day, even though lying down and lazing around are the last things a sick person needs. How they are force-fed suspicious drugs, in fact poisons and narcotics that dull immunity and self-defense mechanisms. We have fallen so low that the disease is perceived as a crime, it is easily just guilt. But not the guilt of the sick but of the healthy.

Our hospitals are prisons where the knowledge of that guilt is interred.

Fyodor Mikhailovich! Batyushka! Let us go to war on reality. You, only you and your genius, your talent, charisma, and influence, can kindle the fire of a righteous revolution of the sick. Otherwise: we will have a revolution of idolaters of health. I saw it all in my visions. Don't dismiss it lightly: that's Parkinson's delirium. That would be a mistake. I have nothing to do with it. I just observed. It may look like delirium, it may be delirium, but it will very soon be a Russian reality. Visions are actually no longer necessary. As an experienced patient and a man of genius, you certainly follow the signs of the times and notice that the increase in concern for people's health (what a fat lie!) makes those same people more and more sick. Each new hospital results in one new fictional disease. Under the layers of these fictitious (but no less unpleasant) diseases, we are no longer able to recognize our real disease unto death; all therapies are therefore wrong and contraindicated, because our true illness contains a cure in itself.

That is—repentance.

Just as Moses rose up against carved and engraved images, you should lead the uprising against the idols of false diseases. It is urgently necessary that you write a masterpiece. A novel that will contain all of Russia. A novel that will perfectly overlay the territory of the Motherland. A novel in which the heroes will be all dead and living Russians. You simply must write the future of Russia. Because if things are left to chance, Russia will turn into a penal colony. And our children will live in the middle of my visions.

Or in the middle of delirium, if you like.

Of course, such an endeavor, writing such a novel that would encompass the entire Russian reality and save it from the destructive influences of the West, from the introduction of new units of measurement, atheism, calendar changes, innovations in spelling and similar things, such a job requires a lot of money and a huge team of assistants. Money should not be a problem. Namely, for some time now, apart from my property, I have been selling other people's property in several surrounding provinces. To finance the work on your novel and to save those estates. As I said, the property will be taken away from their owners very soon and turned into godless cooperatives if our project somehow fails. If it succeeds, the properties will be rightfully returned to their owners.

In addition, there is an alchemist, Khalakhurov, in my summer house, who works on turning base metals into gold. So far, there have been no significant successes. But we are hoping for a breakthrough. In any case, do not worry about money.

In anticipation of your consent to embark on this saving work together,

Yours sincerely,

L. A. Parkinson

Dostoyevsky reads Parkinson's letter with enthusiasm. I would not like to claim that the idea of turning Russia into a novel did not capture his imagination. We won't go that far. Despite his syrupy pretentiousness, he is a remarkable novelist. Ambitious and vain, of course. The execution of Parkinson's idea would ensconce him at the center of Russian cosmogony. Yes, and the tsar would have to do only what he, Dostoyevsky, wrote. Fyodor Mikhailovich immediately answered Lavrentiy Akakyevich. The letter has not been preserved, unfortunately.

Dear Lavrentiy Akakyevich,

Your letter made me unusually happy and restored my faith in the Russian people. I know of your long-standing desire for me to mention you in a novel, and I greatly appreciate your understanding of my principle of not inserting real people in prose. You know very well, Lavrentiy Akakyevich, what we Russians are like. You are absolutely right. If I were to mention someone, say you, it would lead to an avalanche of similar demands. I am not sure if I would dare to resist. There are some powerful people in question . . . Governors, their superiors . . . I hope you understand.

The end result would be a complete profanation of art.

I read with great care the part of your letter that refers to the holy war of the sick against the healthy. As a critically ill man, I am personally interested in that issue. As for the novel, a large-scale work that would encompass all of Russian reality, I have long been thinking of starting work on it. As you correctly guessed, the lack of money for such an all-encompassing job has been the only obstacle to getting down to work.

Now that you have generously solved that problem, however, I am ready to start writing. Tomorrow already.

So, send money.

We will stay in touch.

Sincerely yours,

F. M. Dostoyevsky

According to the story spread in the Russian emigration, apparently intended to save the face of a great writer, Dostoyevsky embarked on the impossible job, giving up only after months and months of hard work and the accompanying terrible nervous exhaustion, which he tried to cure in the casino. More reliable data, which do not diminish the literary significance of Fyodor Mikhailovich, however, are more prosaic and unequivocally claim that having received an enormous money transfer from Mitrofanovsk, Dostoyevsky, instead of starting, actually stopped writing, immediately got on the train, and went to Marienbad (or a similar place), where he was to spend a fabulous sum over three nights, indirectly ruining the future of unknown people whose properties Lavrentiy Akakyevich had sold, as well as the future of their children, many of whom would tragically end up as orphans by the pale fire in the already described frozen forest.

Epilogue, if an epilogue makes sense at all: All revolutions, even those in literature, are not able to change anything and always gamble away whatever is invested in them. After all these years, the path taken by the younger Parkinson seems much better to me. The path to the spiritualization of disease. Because, even if Demyan Lavrentyevich never existed (there is still no consensus on whether he existed or not), it is quite certain that his disease really does exist and that we all, to a greater or lesser extent, suffer from it.

1991. The literary journal *Literaturnaja gazeta* prints the second part of Parkinson's *The History of My Disease.*

D. L. Parkinson

THE HISTORY OF MY DISEASE

PART TWO

When they lost the trail (as they did of me), the later pseudo-biographers gladly assigned my frequent changes of identity to my unwillingness to face harsh criticism of my writings. And yet they did not have a clear idea of what I really wrote, what others wrote under my name, and what, on the other hand, was never written. Which, truth be told, I don't know for sure either. Newspaper lampoon writers went a step further and criminalized those identity changes; so, ostensibly, if they were to be believed, I was hiding from creditors and prosecutors. The truth is quite the opposite. Ever since the pioneering days of parkinsonism, a theological, medical, legal, and police offensive was raised against me. It was not my vanity that was threatened, but my freedom. But, tragic and magnificent at the same time, such is the fate of all who have a mission. In my youthful naivety, convinced that the world was ready to accept the truth, far from knowing that the ignorance and stupidity of the world were intentional, I began to interpret my ideas and write articles in magazines. Already my first, let's call it a lecture, which I gave drunk in that village tavern of enlightenment, cost me a heavy beating, an even heavier bad conscience, and the whole amount from my father's alleged fraudulent sale of property. The devil made me, so drunk, climb on the table and address the patrons. I don't remember exactly what I said. But it must not have been much different from what I normally say. In any case, the men, the landlords, the tavern whores, the servants—they all threw themselves at me in unison and started kicking me, hitting me with spoons, belts and, if I'm not mistaken, bedpans. I guess to humiliate me as much as possible. But they did not humiliate me. To the contrary, the convinced me of the truthfulness of my disease.

My articles in magazines, at first accepted with enthusiasm, like all innovations, soon provoked the anger of the medical guild. Those gentlemen who make careers and accumulate wealth on the terrible sufferings of people, could not calmly watch their offices, clinics, and practices collapse like towers of cards in the wake of my deadly pen. They had to react quickly. To raise those towers again with the help of state coercion. What else could I have expected? What doctor, anywhere in this world, would allow disease to be demystified, let health be put in its rightful place, or have their evil science revealed as a farce? Which medicine essentially is. No, they could not come to terms with the spread of my healing teachings. Already the first sentence of the *Treatise on Illness and Health* (which quickly found its way onto the index of forbidden books)—*Anyone who offers healing, and is not Jesus or one of the twelve apostles, is the most common fraud*—brought them into a state of uncontrolled rage. Not to mention the parts of the treatise in which it is meticulously proven that 99.5% of all disease is the commonplace invention of doctors and pharmacists. Pharmacist hits, as they were later called, mystified the matter even more. This is how it is. Basically, there is only one disease—the disease of life—which I have practically called Parkinson's. All other diseases, and there are no more than four, are just symptoms of Parkinson's disease. Weakness, however, makes every increase in temperature and pressure, every swelling and every pimple be unjustifiably declared a disease, even though these are superficial changes in the state of our poor health. (Take the example of high blood pressure as a typical example of a fictitious disease. Pressure is primarily a physical, not a physiological phenomenon. It should be dealt with by hydraulics, not medicine. When the pressure in a locomotive boiler rises, no one thinks it is a malfunction. The most stubborn stoker knows that the increase in pressure is the result of overheating in the furnace and immediately stops shoveling coal. The engineer, if the needle on the pressure gauge goes into the red, lets off some steam. The engineers of our organism, professed doctors, mumble something about how the patient should devour less bacon and French toast, and always, in consultation with a nearby "pharmacist," prescribes powders or tinctures, instead of following the procedure of the master train engineer and releasing a liter or two of blood from the "patient.")

That's not disease. Here we are dealing with minor mechanical failures.

Disease is something different.

Let's take surgery. Appendicitis, conjunctivitis, benign tumors—all of these are not diseases but mechanical failures. Not only is it incorrect, but it is also dangerous to confuse body mechanics with the metaphysical nature of true disease.

The sickest is the one who thinks he is sick, and he is not.

How did the doctors of that time frown and rage at the lines in which I presented the exact classification of the disease? How they just had to be shocked by the irrefutable evidence that there are only four diseases: weakness, abscesses, inflammation, and cancer! And that all four are in fact just symptoms of integral Parkinson's disease. The first (weaknesses) are dominated by the element of air; the second, (abscesses) the element of water; the third (inflammation) the element of fire, and the fourth (cancer) the element of earth. Heart failure, heart murmurs, myocardial infarction, liver cirrhosis, kidney "diseases," endocrine diseases and the like are among the weaknesses, and they are in fact the only disease that, if treatment is already to be undertaken (which I do not recommend) should be treated with herbs and mineral preparations dominated by the element of air. Quite logically, extremely strong people suffer from the disease of weakness. It is therefore best not to treat them at all. Most doctors know this well. But if they agree, then that is the end of cardiology, internal medicine, nephrology, and endocrinology. The end of a multitude of lucrative jobs.

On a deeper level, however, that division ceases to be valid and diseases again fork into innumerable varieties. No two diseases are the same. The hepatitis that Akakiy Davidovich suffers from is not even histologically similar to the hepatitis that David Akakyevich suffers from. Hepatitis here is just a symbolic community of the sick . . .

But doctors are exceptionally powerful people. It is dangerous to underestimate them. Who else but a doctor can order the tsar to squat or breathe deeply? Who else but a doctor dares to tap the tsar on the chest and knees? Is there anyone else who would dare to shove a finger in the ass of the secret police chief? And to be richly rewarded for doing so. During visits and examinations of various hypochondriac bluebloods, Moscow and St. Petersburg doctors insidiously criticize my doctrine. "Your Highness, Platon Matveyevich, Demyan Parkinson is spreading the teaching that the empire is sick unto death." "I beg your pardon, Inokentiy Pavlovich?" "You heard me right. He claims that Mother Russia is dying. That only a revolution can bring about a resuscitation."

Platon Matveyevich, whoever he is, immediately calls secretaries, undersecretaries, bailiffs, clerks. They hold a closed meeting. The pen scratches. Couriers deliver sealed letters through the labyrinths of the state administration. One copy to the secret police. The second to the cadaster. The third to the imperial censors. The fourth who knows where. A network woven of forgery, rumor, and misinformation is tightening around Mitrofanovsk. My father, Lavrentiy Akakyevich, it is true, sells property. He, however, rightly thinks that they are his properties. And he has no idea that those properties in the cadaster have been transferred into the names of other people. Who have no idea about it. The Russian nobility does not deal with trivial issues of property. They despise money. And they will therefore be left without their properties and money. Because, the problem is not that the conspiracy of doctors and hypochondriacs will send my father into exile; he desires exile and is working hard to find himself there. The problem of Russia, of the whole world, finally, is the volatile nature of lies. The lie, in fact, cannot be controlled. It tends to break away from the liars and act on its own. To cause consequences that liars do not expect at all.

For example: the lie about my alleged revolutionary character abruptly broke all ties with the authors and authorities, and began an independent life in the underground of the capital. Later revolutionaries, the future Mensheviks, Bolsheviks, and Socialist-Revolutionaries, had no idea about the revolution at that time. Those who are more educated vaguely speculate that the word refers to some astronomical phenomenon. These are mostly drunkards, syphilitics, enthusiasts, and bums, who dream of agrarian reform and the right to vote for women. They would forever continue to lead futile debates in taverns so that, as if out of nowhere, rumors about Parkinson's theory about the disease of the empire and the necessity of revolution would not reach those same taverns. An ambitious Siberian treasury officer, V. Ulyanov, already has a construction ready. He listed all the injustices. He designed the correction of each of them. But he wants the impossible: he would like to carry out his reforms within the framework of the imperial order. However, none of that work would have happened if he had not met Merezhkovsky (not the writer, but the musician Merezhkovsky) during his stay in Moscow, who was spreading rumors about the Parkinson's revolution at lunch.

I already knew then that the revolution has nothing to do with politics, that it is a disease; that loud slogans—equality, agrarian reform, freedom, socialism—are mere nonsense in the fever of insidious parkinsonism D. I am fully aware that the revolution cannot be prevented by state terror and police methods but only by medical prophylaxis. But how, when Western medicine, uncritically transferred to Russian soil, is the basic cause and transmitter of the revolutionary disease. When Russian health care is nothing but organizations for the systematic violation of God's commandments. Better if I don't even mention Russian doctors. That guy, Anton Pavlovich, writes stories and theater plays. Ivan Demidovich buys dead souls in the provinces. Pavel Nikolayevich builds houses and rents them out . . .

I see the only way out in the fusion of medicine and theology and in the merging of medical practice and monasticism.

I sent a letter to the Imperial Duma with a proposal for the Law on Health Reform.

They did not even deign me an answer.

I wrote a letter to Nikolai Fyodorov, an ascetic, the author of the famous work *Philosophy of the Common Task.*

Most Respected Nikolai Fyodorovich,

I am taking the liberty of asking you to support an idea whose implementation will improve the spiritual and physical health of the people. It is about the urgent need for the Russification of Western medicine, which has lately been uncritically, too easily taken over from the West. As a military doctor with great experience, and based on extensive research, I responsibly claim: Russian diseases are not the same as European. I do not deny that many of the symptoms of most diseases coincide. The symptoms, however, are external. And focusing attention on the exterior, on the visible manifestations of the disease, on mere changes in the tissues, is the key shortcoming of Western medicine steeped in the most vulgar materialism. To a Russian man, who is essentially an idealist even when he is a convinced supporter of materialist doctrines, such medicine is not able to help the body composition of a Russian. Instead of curing him, such medicine turns him into a caricature of Westerners. Russia needs authentic medical science, and we can reach this only through radical reforms that include merging medical and theological studies.

You certainly know that there are only mental illnesses in Russia. That does not mean that all Russians are crazy. Far from it. If, for example, the case of tuberculosis in a Frenchman is a consequence of poor nutrition and contact with bacteria, in Russia (where there are no bacteria) tuberculosis is contracted either by zeal that is not according to God's will, or by duplicity, as N. D. Guryev established long ago. In Russia, diseases are only a physical expression of the state of the soul. Ulcers, abscesses, spasms, inflammation, catarrh—all these are just materialized sins. Diabetes, tuberculosis, diseases of internal organs—only embodied passions. None of the above should be treated; the attention of an experienced physician must be directed to the pathology of the soul. When sins are eradicated and the passions are cleansed, all other wounds heal on their own.

Modern medicine, as you also know, does not recognize the existence of the soul and thus turns into a hotbed of debauchery and vice. The matter is further aggravated by the fragmentation of integral medical skill, its division into specializations and sub-specializations. Valuable and documented research by the already mentioned N. D. Guryev brings to light devastating findings. Gastroenterologists are all gluttons; internists—arrogant; gynecologists and venereologists—prostitutes; surgeons—incendiaries; orthopedists—misers.

Future Russian doctors must be monks. And they must be sick with all diseases and cure themselves of all of them in order to be able to cure others.

Dear Nikolai Fyodorov, I ask you to invest your reputation and authority in carrying out this noble idea.

With highest regards, R
D. L. Parkinson

Nikolai Fyodorov also did not respond. Later I found out why. He had been dead for ten years, and no one even knew it.

1993. The Belgrade journal of literature and culture *Reč* publishes fragments of the *Tractatus antiheliocentricus,* entitled *The Ideology of Heliocentrism.*

By discovering ancient manuscripts which, by the way, no one ever hid and which were constantly in circulation, Renaissance free thinkers introduced pagan science into Christian civilization, justifying themselves by claiming that science was by nature universal and independent of religious conceptions, which is incorrect. Science originally originated precisely from cults, more precisely from the perversion of cults, and carries within itself the indelible stamp of the religious system under whose auspices it originates. The foundation on which Western civilization was built was not ancient Greece but Christianity. Consequently, Western science should have been based on the Middle Eastern tradition in which Christianity also originated. Instead of a logical choice according to the spiritual, in the Renaissance a choice was made according to racial and geographic proximity. Thus, a horizontally oriented science based on a decimal mathematical system unsuitable for the Christian *weltanschauung* and an even more unsuitable Euclidean geometry was forcibly transplanted into the fabric of a vertical culture, completely suppressing the more appropriate sexagesimal calculus, whose relics are found in dividing time into weeks of seven days and into years of twelve months. Over the last few centuries, pagan science, instead of being brought into accord with the ethical, religious system, has subjugated the religious system to itself. It will not be long till the day when the Pope, in the name of the Catholic Church, will by decree recognize Darwin's theory of evolution as correct.

***

Modern history shapes basic education, that is, a set of things that are taken for granted, through proclamations by which certain events, phenomena and personalities are declared "positive," "negative," "advanced," or "backward." Thus, Middle Eastern mathematics and technology were *a priori* denounced as obscure and magical pseudoscience, unworthy of the attention of the Enlightenment, in which, miraculously, millions of people found a relevant guide for decision-making in meaningless horoscopes published in newspapers, often compiled not according to the position of the stars, but according to current political needs. However, many technical relics of Middle Eastern civilization, such as the pyramids, for example, are still a mystery to enlightened scientists even on the level of construction methods, not to mention the complete unknown of the meaning of the system of large buildings scattered across the Egyptian deserts.

***

An example of history as a political pamphlet can be found in the *Encyclopaedia Britannica* under the heading "Renaissance." In histories dealing with a specific topic, ideological speech is diluted by meanders of great narration and layers of statistical data. In the encyclopedic text, however, where a limited amount of space is available to summarize the mass of data, we find nothing but data that's relevant, not even for the policies of the time, but exclusively for the needs of modern political ideology. The period called the Renaissance, taken for itself, is a fragment of the passage of time, neither better nor worse than any other. Only the subsequently ideologized Renaissance, created in offices at the end of the eighteenth century, is fatal, just as idealized and ideologized antiquity, also created in offices in the Renaissance, proved to be subversive to the later course of history.

"The Renaissance 'rebirth,'" it says in *Britannica*:

> . . . period in European civilization immediately following the Middle Ages and conventionally held to have been characterized by a surge of interest in Classical scholarship and values. The Renaissance also witnessed the discovery and exploration of new continents, the substitution of the Copernican for the Ptolemaic system of astronomy . . . the growth of commerce, and the invention or application of such potentially powerful innovations as paper, printing, the mariner's compass, and gunpowder. To the scholars and thinkers of the day, however, it was primarily a time of the revival of Classical learning and wisdom after a long period of cultural decline and stagnation."

***

We see that in the enumeration of the achievements of the Renaissance, what will later be called the Copernican Revolution, that is, the replacement of the geocentric image of the world with a heliocentric model, occupies a high place. This revolution indirectly and in the long run caused a series of dramatic changes in the Western world, in fact splitting it into two separate, qualitatively completely different civilizations: vertical, Christian; and horizontal, technological, paradoxically realizing the ideals of the Renaissance only in recent times. The geometrization of urban forms, the obsessive care for the body, emphasized interest in athletic disciplines (sports), the rise of despised professions, the flourishing of syncretistic cults, and the emancipation of homosexuality, all connect the modern age with the Hellenic world in a declining phase. The Renaissance, therefore, is not the beginning of a new age, but the twilight of a vertical Christian civilization, whose disintegration was to last until the Enlightenment and the French Revolution.

***

The heliocentric theory at first glance only corrects one omission of perception and puts the relations between celestial objects in their rightful place. If we agree that the geocentric system is a consequence of an error in perception, the theory is flawless. But precisely from the point of view of perception, to the claim that the Earth is at the center of the universe and that the entire celestial vault revolves around it, no objection can be made: direct sensory experience assures us that it is so. Heliocentric theory, after all, is not calculated so much to execute a revolution in astronomy as in psychology. Its spread and acceptance laid the foundations for the loss of faith in direct experience, and the redirection of trust to an external authority that denies God's existence and puts secularized science in its place.[12]

***

This great relocation, however, is of no significance for practical relations in the external space. For the human world, but also for technology, it is completely irrelevant what it revolves around; whether the center is the Earth or the Sun. After all, the Theory of Relativity will show that "within the same system it is not possible

12. It is interesting to mention that in the practical application of astronomy, in navigation for example, things are set up so that the Earth is the center of the universe.

to determine what moves in relation to what" and that in a curved space, similar to the surface of a ball, no center is possible in the strict sense. Traditional teachings place the Earth at the center of the universe at a level that is incomparably more important than the interrelationships of celestial bodies, and that assumes that physical space is only a relative phenomenon to which a higher degree of reality is superior. Geocentrism symbolically indicates man's medial position in the hierarchy of the universe, in which human consciousness is the point of contact of the visible and invisible world. By expelling the Earth from the center of the universe in a psychological sense, the Copernican revolution returns the human world to the authority of determinism, at the same time introducing a series of nomadic and solar cults, disguised by the formulations of impartial science.

From then on, we are no longer the inhabitants of the center of the universe, but creatures that inhabit an insignificant planet lost in the ugly infinity of physical space. This made a break in the hierarchical energy currents of the universe and the processes of insubordination spread unhindered downward, gradually destroying all forms of life based on stable, traditional models. By depriving man of faith in immediate experience and deafening itself to the authority of the scriptures, heliocentric theory paved the way for a growing derealization.

***

The decadence of the city begins with the demolition of the city walls, its original institutions. Nomadic attacks destroyed the walls from the outside, but they were always rebuilt; the modern age brought something new: a diffuse siege from the inside.

The tendency conceived in the Renaissance to easily qualify certain phenomena as "progressive" (as if progression cannot take any direction) announced a subversive process of destroying the city by "opening," implying that "openness" is also something *a priori* positive. The demolition of city walls in the first place means the removal of borders, not only in the urban-architectural sense, but the removal of all borders in general, opening the door to the expansion of horizontal freedom which, deprived of formation and direction restrictions, was to end in the current chaos.

***

The orientation of the perception of quantity has led to the statistical increase in urban population being accepted as a reliable indicator of progress, although it is quite clear that urban sprawl means increasing urban problems and, more dangerously, rural collapse, which in a relatively short time, because of exhaustion, has the effect of the subsequent impoverishment of cities.

The metastases of cities as an expression of confusion in space have their origins in the epistemological confusion caused by diverting attention from the vertical axis to the horizontal, from theocentrism to anthropocentrism, a diversion that is ideologically shaped in the form of a heliocentric image of the world. Like all ideologies, the ideology of heliocentrism is mimicry; in fact, it is pure egoism, in whose field of vision there is no place for God, except as the "God the Watchmaker," as a disinterested mover of a field of forces over which, once put into operation, he has no influence whatsoever.

***

The gnoseological confusion inevitably led to terminological confusion. Gradually, a conceptual system was built in which certain concepts were declared absolute values, and others lost their significance again. Freedom, equality, human rights, for example, are suddenly set as absolute values; due to growing superficiality this is accepted without resistance, although freedom, equality or human rights do not exist as something isolated, as a quality, but are a relation, and their quality depends on the nature of the relation. Thus, we return to the problem of the border, because it is the border that gives freedom form and meaning, as is the case in a vertically organized society in which spatial and ethical constraints serve as kinds of "walls" that direct energies upwards. These constraints were certainly broken before the city walls were torn down because the insurmountable aspiration to the infinite, once redirected from the vertical and inner to the horizontal and outer, had to find expression in the expansion and removal of constraints, which represented a kind of repeated Eastern sin and the Babylonianization of the world, because in that way not only the limit set by God was crossed, but also the limits set by nature. This is the very essence of what we call alienation: a state of derealization in which man is equally distant from God and from nature.

***

In a metaphysical sense, a city that has transcended its boundaries ceases to be a city in the traditional sense and transitions to the state that preceded the construction of the fortification—a kind of urbanized steppe ruled by a nomadic spirit. That spirit uses the conveniences of civilization, the comfort of city life above all, but rejects the limitations that traditional city life presupposes. Instead of traditional forms, ceremonies, processions, and carnivals—closely related to the calendar, climate, and change of seasons—an order of chance and impermanence is introduced, from which phenomena such as fashion, sports spectacles, tourism, and other barely concealed forms of the nomadic spirit emerge in modern times.

Closely related to the decadence of the city is the alienation of time. As the world's attention shifted from the inner-vertical to the outer-horizontal, time lost its subjective quality and gradually turned into a physical size. Then they started measuring, parceling, a kind of specification of time, creating a very dangerous, but difficult to grasp illusion of the spread of time. Thus, time grew into a precursor to an external force, into a kind of apparatus of coercion, because the control of space is now based on the manipulation of the time dimension, that is, on the premeditated arrangement of events or their forced provocation. However, the quantification and ideologization of space, time, and technological acceleration due to discrepancies with the natural order of things, create a rift and tension between the world of man and the world of nature.

***

The open city of modernity, a city whose walls were destroyed by internal occupation, is similar to an open wound and becomes subject to subversive influences, which this time do not come from the outer space but from itself. The industrial age created a multiplied need for labor, which the existing human resources could not satisfy, and so there were large migrations from the countryside to the cities. If we observe these migrations independently of ideological and economic implications, they openly appear to be invasions, spontaneous movements of the masses which, if we abstract the utilitarian dimension, bring with them destruction and devastation as necessary consequences of the invasion. Similarly, the expansion of industrial production in which these masses participate also represents a form of devastation, because expansion is a slow-moving explosion. The civilization of the city is thus exposed to a series of implosions and explosions, which are ideologically presented as progress and technological advancement.

The decentralization of social relations and the weakening of the vertical, class structure of society is becoming visible on the urban level. Migration as an implosion leads to the destruction of the structure of the traditional city which is directed towards the center (agora, cathedral). The city center very quickly became a mere administrative term, because within an agglomeration whose periphery cannot be determined (because there are no more walls), it is not possible for any *topos* to impose itself as a natural center towards which city activities are inclined. The current chaos of the megalopolis is therefore conditioned by metaphysical necessity. Devastation, loneliness, the law of the stronger are not deviations but the law of the megalopolis which, undermined from within, becomes an urbanized steppe.

***

The egalitarian tendencies articulated in the French Revolution, as we will find out in a subsequent analysis, did not aim to establish equality among people, which is impossible, but the abolition of the vertical structure of society and class, shaping and directing factors of civilized life in general. The French Revolution, on the other hand, is much more an ontological, epistemological, and semantic revolution than a social revolution. By introducing a new reckoning of time, the French Revolution showed a strong desire for discontinuity and the total rejection of tradition, while denying God, even as "God the Watchmaker" and placing a naked prostitute on the throne in Notre Dame Cathedral as the personification of reason. Coincidentally or not, instead of a seamstress, housewife, or woman from the people, a prostitute was chosen, which is certainly not without a symbolic connection with the later role of the priest of reason—intellectuals.

***

The next stage of removing borders and abolishing urban and personal privacy confronted the revolutionary processes of "liberation" with a seemingly insurmountable obstacle: the walls of personal habitats which, for understandable reasons, could not simply be destroyed. Bypasses had to be found, a technology that would eliminate the definition and privacy of the habitat, while keeping the walls in place. That's how newspapers come on the scene. These were, first of all, daily newspapers, which were experiencing expansion in the period after the French Revolution and which were creating the beginnings of what would later be called "public opinion," a diffuse set of prejudices, half-truths and mystifications. From then on, the average person does not have to build personal judgments, but can rely on ready-made patterns that fluctuate "public opinion," classifying "good" and "evil," "useful" and "harmful," "beautiful" and "ugly." Since then, thanks to the narrowed view of "public opinion," the world has become seemingly clear, explainable, and logical for the average person; this narrowing gives rise to a tide of scientific optimism and the belief that in the coming decades, science will complete its work, creating one variant of the world as the Garden of Pleasures. Such a mood was the starting point for the emergence of later utopian doctrines, which were not recognized as utopian in the passive mental environment, mainly due to the fact that they were supported by "public opinion."

***

After the city walls were demolished, the social pyramid was destroyed, that is, the boundaries between the classes were removed. It was not easy to resist the seductiveness of this endeavor, which at first sight corresponds to the Christian idea of equality and which, also at first sight, reflects the deepest human resistance to injustice. However, the processes of desacralization always misinterpret and simplify sacral forms, so equality and equality before the law in the ontological sense—in which both the greatest saint and the greatest sinner are equally precious to God—was literally transferred to the social plane and now it is common to think that everyone is equally good and equally gifted to do any job. This produced a rebellion against the hierarchical order, which was often unjust, but was the only thing that ensured the more or less harmonious development of society.

***

The destruction of the vertical social structure resulted in a somewhat strange phenomenon: the gradual egalitarianization of social relations did not lead to raising all strata to a higher level but to a general decline in which the worst traits prevail, leading to the need to create verification systems, written obligations, accounting, and detailed criminal laws. The human word lost all value. Today, it has gone so far that, except in England, a statement about one's own identity is not taken for granted, but is verified by a legitimizing document in which the state guarantees the identity of a certain person. This decline is clearly seen in the example of the degradation of war. In a vertical society, war is the job of a special class and is mostly reduced within the boundaries of a group of professional warriors, and the state of war is in a sense only one of the activities of society, whose normal course is rarely disturbed. In addition, war is spatially limited and, like everything else, horizontally static, reduced to the personal struggle of its participants in which courage, skill, and strength are crucial. The modern age, by introducing firearms, democratizes and dehumanizes warfare, because with the use of weapons that are effective at a distance, anyone, regardless of courage and skill, can kill an opponent who is now, due to that distance, reduced to a purely statistical size. Very quickly, everything that was recently considered a disgrace and dishonor unworthy of a warrior, that is, an attack, an ambush, became a virtue or even the science of tactics. The development of the artillery, on the other hand, made the city walls an outdated means of protection, and long sieges and bombings, the totalization of the war began, in which civilians were now being killed more and more often.

***

The next phase of the city's decline is the introduction of roads within its core. In the traditional city, the roads, which were directed to the north, south, east, and west, ended at the city gates. Thus, the turmoil of the world remained outside the walls. Under the pretext of improving communication and simplifying the loading and unloading of goods, roads (and then railways) enter the city core and disrupt the statics of urban life, turning cities into roadside taverns. Now, the "class of utilitarianism and secularism is entering the historical scene victoriously, considering the greatest enjoyment and the least work to be the highest good, as a result of which it rejects as unnecessary everything that does not directly serve that goal." (N. Fyodorov)

***

Immediately after the establishment of the nation-states, politics ceased to be politics in its original sense. Because politics, as absurd as it may seem now, is incompatible with ideology. The mixing of religion and politics was already yielding poor results; but religion remained religion, and politics remained politics. The interference of ideology as a substitute for religion in political matters, in conjunction with the absolutist tendencies of ideology, created a monstrous amalgam; speaking in *Buddhist* terminology, it produced another layer of *Maya,* a veil of illusion, in addition to the one present in the very structure of nature. This meant the beginning of researching nature with the help of fictitious, falsified, at best relative, parameters and apparatuses. The gnoseological failure of the modernist research project is less important here; what is worrying is the negative impact of scientific theories on the structure of reality, on general phenomena understood extremely primitively as a field of phenomena independent of human ideas about them.[13]

13. It would certainly be interesting to compare the processes of social atomization with the discoveries of subatomic physics and quantum theory. Or the increase in general consumption with the increase in energy production.

***

According to traditional teachings, the universe and man (as a small universe) are structured hierarchically, i.e. vertically.[14]

The very idea of hierarchy, however, came out in a very bad light thanks to the relentless ideological propaganda of modernist doctrines, which saw in it a theoretical justification for the rule of one "class" over others, although modern doctrines created this artificial division. Yet Plato, in his analysis of society, classified capitalists and workers in the same class of producers; these people are, regardless of the material differences between them, connected by the interest of production, technique, sales, and purchase. On the social ladder, they are, regardless of material circumstances, situated at the bottom. In vertically structured societies, ancient and Christian, for example, this position is in no way humiliating, because it is a matter of choice, inclination and ability. Unlike modern materialism, in class societies, both materials and bodies have an incomparably higher status.

***

Class communities are not organized ideologically but energetically; politics, we have already said, used to be just a city management technique, a skill completely lost over time: a kind of mixture of urbanism, logistics and defense engineering, which, with the exception of the strategist, was entirely in the hands of the producer class. Politics is, therefore, a producing activity. Politics in the modern sense of the word did not yet exist; in its place was strategy: the technique of

14. The very word "universe," composed of *unum* and *inversum*, etymologically indicates verticality and a starting unity.

defending the city. What even the smallest Mediterranean city had, today not even the greatest powers have. But the absence of strategy or, worse, the presence of fictitious strategies, not only makes the global order meaningless; it brings disorder to both the domain of tactics and tactical logistics. The huge number of delays, non-functionalities, technical and traffic accidents, which everyday life is full of, testifies more to the crisis of the concept of physical reality than to the imperfection of technologies. For insufficiently clear reasons, appearance—time and space, movement and form—are taken as unchangeable qualities, despite the commonsense fact that they are the causes of instability and change. Change, however, is not a catastrophe *per se* until it collides with the rigid notions and prejudices we have about what kind of course it should take. These prejudices are woven from things that wish to present themselves as being devoid of prejudices: from pseudo-exactness and rigid logical systems. In that light, the main cause of delays and accidents, for example with trains, is the timetable, an abstract schedule that defies permanent and subtle changes of appearance until that moment, that critical point where the system breaks down and where trains collide. This applies to all systems, especially political ones. Social reality is conditioned by a multitude of microsystems within the basic one, which is what is called social ordering in the pseudoscience of sociology. But that is basically a more subtle form of architecture; the architecture of the city is only its material expression. The system of social hierarchy, rules, etiquette, and conventions is a building in the literal sense. It is represented by a class society in which each class and each individual knows their place in the social structure; social construction does not function well without the cooperation and complementarity of all classes; they must all be present in order for society to last and prosper.

***

Changes happen long before they become obvious, both in physical and social reality, and not even for a moment should we lose sight of the fact that these two realities are closely connected, that they are, moreover, just different manifestations of the same reality. Neglecting social architecture over time leads to it becoming like a timetable: an abstract series of regulations and forms that, unfulfilled in content, after a period of inertia lead to revolution as a catastrophe, revolution as the collapse of social reality to a lower, temporarily stable level. By their nature, revolutions are akin to tectonic catastrophes; what floods and earthquakes are for nature, revolution is for society. Human actions have a decisive influence on both, hence the unusual phenomena—earthquakes, comets, epidemics, etc.—are not predictions of great catastrophes but part of a catastrophic process. However, for some reason, only the social dimension of human activities is taken into consideration, although they also equally undermine the sphere of the material world.

It is the compression of matter and spirit, body and soul, nature and abstraction, into the same, horizontal plane; then, the imposition of autonomy on all of the above, which is the basic misconception of modernism, masks the vertical structure of the universe in which each state originates from the higher and more subtle, at the same time merging with the lower and more primitive. The world becoming atheist is at the same time its dematerialization and derealization. Without a spiritual dimension, matter, which has been given a high place in Christian optics, is reduced to ore, to building material, rubble or, in recent times, pollution.

In parallel with the introduction of divisions into things and phenomena that are complementary, insisting on further analysis instead of synthesis, modernism has exerted a subversive influence on the notion of time and space, and thus on space and time themselves. It has gone so far that the surface is regularly identified and mixed with space. But space is not a physical size, it is a mode of perception; it is the hidden quality of the surface and the bodies that fill it, placed in close connection with time manifested as duration.

The externalization of space and time is their politicization, the expropriation of spread and duration. At that stage, politics radically moves away from its original function and grows into a center of power that manipulates the duration and spread of both physical greatness and people. Such politics, brought to its extreme consequences, is totalitarianism: an order in which duration is subjected to rigorous supervision, in which all places are public, and movement is strictly controlled. The system of concentration camps, therefore, is not the dark side of such orders, but their ideal: everyone in the place prescribed by the state, subordinated to the prescribed time schedule, which is expressed by a seemingly tempting slogan—eight hours of work, eight hours of entertainment, eight hours of rest. It is a Timetable on a global scale. However, the attempt to impose this abstract order on reality, seemingly paradoxically, will end in a dramatic increase in chaos.

***

In the search for the causes of the crisis in which it finds itself from the very beginning, modern thinking rarely goes far into the past, nor does it wonder whether that thinking itself is the cause of the crisis. It mostly moves within a period of at most some fifty years back. The modern analysis of the past suffers from hopeless modern centrism; its excursions into history are burdened by the transfer of the conceptual apparatus and mental patterns of modernity to epochs that were based on diametrically opposed patterns, completely different technologies, and different foundations. Everything that is inconsistent with modernist optics is declared barbarism, ignorance, and backwardness. That is the tactic of historical politics: at all costs to create the impression that we live in a privileged epoch, at the peak of history, in the realization of a modern utopia. Hence the importance of historiography, a significance that it did not have in earlier epochs. In ancient Greece, for example, history had the function of entertaining reading, reportage; history still retained its original role in its name, which literally means "narrative."

***

In a strict sense, reality is nothing but a story and all that can be said about it is a narration. This was the case until the beginning of the modern age, in which, overnight, exactness prevailed over the aesthetic, and common sense over the imagination. However, a slightly deeper analysis of the exactness of science and history reveals that it is of a purely intratextual nature, that it has a rhetorical effect; ultimately, it is a matter of style. The only thing that is exact here is the tone, and that tone, paradoxically, counts on the inaccuracy of perception and its tendency towards simplification and generalization. Precision is always in the service of politics. Geographical measurements, for example, refer to idealized surface fragments, without taking into account the morphology of the soil, countless fractals and irregularities which, in practice and in the measurement of soil micro-samples, make it pointless. Measurement mania, however, has no scientific or practical significance; it is a crypto-political project. It is a matter of secularized numerology, a de-spiritualized Kabbala, a magical procedure, the mimesis of Divine omniscience.

The imposition of the heliocentric model as the authoritative one fundamentally changed man's position in the universe. One feeling is that man and his Earth are the central point of the universe, the link between the higher dimensions of existence and the material world, but quite another is the idea of the Earth as a satellite of a peripheral star lost in outer space. The acceptance of the heliocentric system as the only credible one has laid the foundations for a modern, desacralized, and secular world in which either chance or destiny reign. However, science thus collides with its own position that within one and the same system it is not possible to determine what is moving in relation to what. After all, it is irrelevant; we operate with notions and facts, and it does not matter whether those facts correspond to an "objective" order. Kant has shown that we cannot know what things and phenomena are in their objectivity; we make judgments about them on the basis of perception and representation. The inauguration of the heliocentric model in a deeper analysis is indicated as the re-establishment of the pagan solar cult and the radical, albeit covert, rejection of monotheism. We find the external forms of this civilizational regression in many modern phenomena, starting from nudism and naturism as the most primitive forms, to the solar emblems of totalitarian ideologies. Forms of sun worship are disguised; being without a sacral and ritual dimension, they exist as a lifestyle. On the other hand, we have the resurrection of obscure, orgiastic cults that correspond to the ancient telluric mysteries. But they are also deprived of any depth, even if it is counter-initiation, and are reduced to a politicized, ideologized sexuality, whose followers become a respectable political force in megalopolises. In general, the characteristic of the modern age is that it sets perversions, intimidation, and arbitrariness, which it produces itself, as political problems that it is called upon to solve.

***

If, as the doctrine of heliocentrism claims, the universe is not organized hierarchically, if it is a random set of celestial bodies lost in meaningless infinity, then why should human society be hierarchically organized? That is the concise ideology of heliocentrism, an ideology that infiltrates all forms of life unnoticed over time. The decline of the monarchy as a way of organizing the human community does not mean, as it is interpreted, the historical downfall of the idea of the monarchy, but the downfall of the people. Or, in the language of architecture: it is no longer possible to build a stable social pyramid from generations to come; from that time onwards, societies became more and more amorphous, as evidenced, among other things, by the devastating shapelessness of modern settlements.

We now see quite clearly that science is not research but the production of the "objective"; not an interpretation but a presentation of reality. We do not notice the artificiality of the current image of the world for the simple reason that we have forgotten by the nature of things that it was learned, because we, like language, spontaneously accepted it while growing up. We experience perception, as well as language, as immanent, however—just as accident determines that our mother tongue is this or that of the linguistic multitude—a completely different perception is also possible, from which a different epistemology and a different aesthetics would automatically emerge. The notion of space, for example, has experienced a metamorphosis over time that can be traced based on a comparison of visual presentations of objects and landscapes, created before the Copernican Revolution and in more recent times. The striking difference in the representation of the same objects in a comic way is justified by the imperfection of the technique of drawing and painting in earlier epochs, despite the claims of painters and art aesthetics that these techniques are superior to today's. On the example of a woodcut from the seventeenth century, on which a group of pyramids is presented, their elongation and emphasized verticality in relation to the pyramids as we know them is striking. Doubts about the artist's skill are pointless; we would rather assume that he saw the pyramids as such and that he drew them faithfully in accordance with his perception, which should be treated equally with the modern perception of the pyramids. Because, all other data, which modern thinking is so proud of, are also quantitative, crypto-magical in nature, based on measurements which, not only in the case of the pyramids, always reduce the object to the geometric abstraction which it resembles and which is the only one available for measurement.

***

Space, its perception, is closely related to the intellectual fashion of an epoch; the impact of what is called common sense on overall reality has not been sufficiently explored. Its prejudices by no means exclusively affect the domain of the intellectual, but actively influence the whole picture of the world. It is able to cause changes in the biological sphere. If we return to the field of sexuality for a moment, we will see that the ideal figure of a woman is closely related to variations of general taste, and that having these ideal figures—not only through cosmetics and dietetics—makes whole generations of girls grow either into curvaceous women or lithe ones, depending on the current taste.

Reality that is not related to the sacral spheres is volatile, elusive, and subject to change; materialist doctrines, scientism, and totalitarianism in politics, therefore, are not the result of any scientific insight, but an expression of an inert desire for stability, for unchanging legitimacy. They are an expression of a faith incomparably more absurd than belief in the resurrecting God. The doctrine of heliocentrism, which over time has grown into an ideology, means a final break with the vertical order of the universe; it is the violent reduction of reality to the phenomenology of one of its segments, the one that the Kabbalistic tradition calls *Malkuth*. By the way, the Kabbalistic interpretation of the origin of the cosmos—in the light of the latest achievements of physics—is incomparably more feasible, even in the optics of common sense, than scientific cosmological theories. Finally, one gets the impression that science does not want to seriously deal with the origin of the world at all, and that the theories that appear here and there are more in the function of a pseudo-mythological completion of the picture of the world than true research. The expulsion of the Earth to the periphery of the universe coincides with the emergence and affirmation of provincial doctrines, of the provincial spirit in general, as well as with the emergence of nation-states and the separation of church and state. This separation has definitely removed the sacral dimension from human everyday life. It is a matter of practical nature: the limitations imposed by religion are incompatible with the modern conception of politics and technology as means of unlimited power. God became superfluous, not because some discerning guy reliably learned that he did not exist but because he wanted himself to be god. That possibility, however, was denied in Eden, when Adam was prevented from eating from the Tree of Life. All efforts in this direction, as a form of counter-initiation, have the opposite effect: instead of progress, ontological regression is obtained; instead of omnipotence, increasing inertia. Religiosity is politicized and sunk into either Caesaropapism or ethno-phyletism, while on the other hand politics is sacralized: one nation, one class or, even, more recently, one sex, is seemingly set as a quasi-metaphysical goal that conceals a regression to the modern pagan cult, to modern Manichaeism, which sees evil in everything but itself. Because when things are reduced, when the illusion of a multitude of possibilities is seen as illusory, we are faced with the fact that the perception of reality can be either religious or magical.

The separation of church and state, one of the civilizational "achievements" of the modern age, is a manifestation of a much more radical separation, the separation of "heaven" and "earth." From then on, human reality has forcibly been reduced to the boundaries of the telluric and the biological, and the abstract "Man" (with a capital M) is enthroned as the measure of all things, which results in a general relativization and the predominance of determinism. We have only recently seen the consequences of this process in all their destructiveness.

***

The separation of church and state, however, is not the last word of modernity. As we have already said, it was a question of separating heaven and earth; it will by no means stop at secularization. This is just the first step. The next is (it can already be seen) the separation of people from the earth in the most literal sense of the word. The final outcome of this process of dissolution will be de-corporation, the dis-incarnation of human beings.

1995. A notebook (intended for wrapping food) with the manuscript of dissident A. P. Mekdonaljd's *Memories of Demyan Lavrentyevich* was accidentally found in a delicatessen in St. Petersburg.

Afksentiy Platonovich Mekdonaljd

MEMORIES OF DEMYAN LAVRENTYEVICH

I gladly respond to the kind invitation to write a few pages about Demyan Lavrentyevich Parkinson, although I am almost certain that the manuscript will be burned, lost or, at best, stored in the Repository of Forbidden Articles and Books. That archive, for which no one knows where it is, conceals in its cellars invaluable spiritual treasure. What Russian literature would be like, crippled even like this by the censorship of the Security Service and the NKVD (which is one and the same), we can only guess. The world would certainly be different if at least some of the banned manuscripts were published. Because all of Slavic civilization was imprisoned in writing in the Archive, which was doomed to ruin from the outset by the insane reforms of the autocrat Peter the First Commander, the transition from the Julian to the Gregorian calendar, and the replacement of the traditional system of measures with the decimal system. The best Russian writers have written and are writing for the Archive. Not for the public. Undoubtedly, Demyan Lavrentyevich Parkinson, a theologian, polymath, successful hotelier and, above all, the inventor of an ingenious disease, is one of those greats.

I met Parkinson in a group of young people, poets, writers, and philosophers, in the circle of the religious thinker Solovyov, for whom it later turned out that he was a spy for the Vatican and was actively working on the project of making Russia into a Uniate country. Parkinson was the first to see through him. "It is indisputable that Solovyov gave great interpretations of the Old Testament," he said dryly. "I do not question his history of theocracy either, but he is essentially only a minor hero of his literature, which combines things that should remain separate, in this case German idealism and Orthodox Christianity, thus only increasing spiritual disarray." Parkinson was inspired by the writings of Isaac of Nineveh, Maximus the Confessor, and Ruysbroeck. He had nothing to look for among the ambitious Moscow philosophers who compose their writings in accordance with the secret inclinations of their patrons. His theology was short and clear: "An old man must die. And he who dies must rot and disintegrate, 'for life to devour death.'" An orderly environment, comfortable homes, legality—none of this goes hand in hand with honest Christians. Who is crazy enough to die and decompose if everything is going well for him, if no one abuses or humiliates him? That is why tsarist Russia, with all its injustices and abominations, is an ideal place to make the leap into the other world. In Russia, strictly speaking, there is no one who is not a monk.

"Here, like it or not, everyone is an ascetic."

In winter of that year (1891?), Demyan Parkinson went through an unusual mystical experience. In a dream, which suddenly turned into a state incomparably more realistic than reality, Jakob Böhme, about whom our hero had never heard before, appeared to him. "When I woke up," (Isaac Babel will be confided in much later), "I couldn't remember most of the things Böhme told me about, but my perceptions changed overnight and I began to think quite differently. I only remembered some unimportant details, probably allegories, such as the parable of the Eternal Prostitute that appears in every generation and is known for having the demonic ability to speak through her anus." Inspired by this event, Demyan Parkinson writes his first apocryphal work in a fever, *The Final Days of Jakob Böhme*, whose authorship he attributes to a fictional person, the alleged mystical apprentice Schwenekpfeld. The writing itself, however, conceived as a literary attempt, will have a strong influence on the pseudo-religious life of Russia. The confused piety of the Moscow suburbs, prone to extremes and exaggerations of all kinds, welcomes like a heavenly gift the small booklet full of Böhme's fantastic feats. The leader of the heresy, which is spreading like a plague among the shoemakers of the capital and their regular customers, became a certain Vsevolod Lavrentyevich Mekdonaljd. I must mention we are not related. I am from the Mekdonaljds of the Tver *guberniya*.) The sect took on a name, paper-eaters, after one of the key dogmas of the heresy whose sacrament is plain paper. The other rules are no less absurd: like the obligation of the faithful to marry the ugliest and most grumpy women or, whenever they can, to attend executions; to be humiliated at every opportunity and to sleep in barns, chicken coops and pig styes, or at least on benches in the workshop.

All religions, authentic or false, have their own mystics, ascetics, and martyrs. Mekdonaljd's sect does not deviate from that rule either. While most members of the sect symbolically eat a piece of paper with a meal, we come across zealous followers who eliminate everything but paper from their diet. If we keep in mind that this humble diet is doused with large amounts of vodka, then it is not surprising that fanaticism reigns in the ranks of the paper-eaters. Mekdonaljd (who, interestingly, is not one of those who feed only on paper) somehow jumps over the abyss between being a shoemaker's journeyman and a theologian, and compiles a confusing booklet, on the pages of which he tries to lay out his theology. According to him, paper made from wood is nothing but a more or less digestible prototype of the Tree of the Knowledge of Good and Evil. Eating paper, its further mystical transformation in the processes of digestion, is nothing but the redemption of ancestral curiosity and self-confidence. Sleeping, on the other hand, among animals, in feces, is a recognition of our true condition, the depth of our depravity. Mekdonaljd strongly condemns the scandalous fashion of bathing, especially everyday bathing, which is slowly gaining supporters in Russia as well. "It will cleanse the exterior and the body," he writes in his gloomy catechism, "but it will pollute God's rivers and seas." (From an ecological point of view, an astonishingly accurate remark: the cleaner we are, the more polluted the environment is.) Later, however, when the persecution of the paper-eaters begins, a trademark of the sect, an unbearable stench, will strike down many honest atheists or Orthodox folk who will be banished only because they stink due to lack of soap or bad habits.

Winter is coming, soles are falling off, there are no *valyenkas* on the market, and Moscow shoemakers are lazing about in their workshops. They pass the time interpreting Mekdonaljd's somnambulant sermons. On Sundays, however, when other citizens doze off after lunch or go to the theaters, the paper-eaters go out to parks and streets; they offer children and hooligans a penny to spit on them or kick them in the buttocks. The Archbishop of Moscow, realizing this was no joking matter, invited Mekdonaljd to the Bishop's Palace for lunch, with the intention of returning him to the fold of golden Orthodoxy. And what came out of all that? Coming from lunch, Mekdonaljd mocked the bishop, describing him as a glutton. With these words, "Oh, brothers, the servants brought out the fried fish.

The sight of the delicious meal pleased His Holiness so much that he stared at the fish with a blissful smile on his face. The fish, even fried like that, couldn't resist either. And it laughed at him."

News of the paper-eating sect finally reached the imperial offices. There, shoemakers were not much respected; Russia was already losing a third war because of bad boots, which fell apart in the first rain. Now they were even neglecting their otherwise sloppy job. Something had to be done. Exile to Siberia seemed like a reasonable solution. Said, done. Mekdonaljd and his followers are sentenced to prison; then they are chained and taken to the railway station, to a train whose terminal station is not yet on the geographical maps of the Empire. Actually, it was not even built yet. But by the time the train arrives, it will be completed. It is worth mentioning that this procession of exiles is part of the punishment in Russia: the procession is slowly passing through the city streets, exposed to ridicule and insults from the crowds. Of course, there are always a few episodic characters of F. M. Dostoyevsky to feel sorry for the poor and to give them a penny or a crust of bread, in order to provide the author with material for his extremely dubious thesis about the "Russian soul." But the mockery has a completely different effect on Mekdonaljd and his followers. They experience it as an expression of God's special mercy, as an outpouring of unexpected grace. Persecution strengthens them in their faith in a certain way. How, after all, do you punish people who sleep in feces and welcome all the hardships of life? Punishments have an effect only on wrongdoers. Instead of eradicating the sect, the Imperial Decree paradoxically makes it stronger. Because, upon arrival in Siberia, they are assigned—by the irony of fate or by imperial officials—to work in a paper mill, in an environment where their heresy flourishes and in which they gain a lot of supporters, which is for Siberia, where at that time besides paper there is not much else to eat, somewhat understandable.

Vsevolod Lavrentyevich Mekdonaljd slipped in the mill one day, fell into a woodchipper, and ended up processed into paper. The sect thus received a martyr and operated until the Great October Revolution, when the people's commissars set out to eradicate all kinds of religiosity with sword and fire. But, in a mysterious way, transmitted by who knows which ways, the heresy of paper-eaters was secretly spreading in Southeast Europe, where, in a slightly changed form, it has been preserved to this day.

In parallel with Vsevolod Mekdonaljd, whom Gogol immortalized in one of his novels, Demyan Parkinson also deals with metaphysics and theology, pretending not to hear rumors from Moscow about a strange sect of paper-eaters following the teachings of the Protestant heretic Böhme. (How else to interpret Parkinson's sentence from a letter to E. Onegin: "It is absolutely impossible to write such a fantastic sentence that will not come true sooner or later.") He thinks intensively about the problem of time, which results in an extensive study signed by Parkinson the elder, who already thinks it's all the same. He can no longer offer other people's property for sale; he sold off three *guberniyas*; what does it mean to him to sign a book he didn't write, which he would never write, especially if he doesn't know about it. Demyan guards his own signature like his worst enemy. "It's enough," he tells a friend, "to sign a paycheck to deserve hell because of pride. So, let's take the example of Fyodor Mikhailovich. He writes with so much warmth about monks, church people in general, maybe he really believes in God, but when he sees his name on the cover of some of his books, that otherwise gentle man turns into a beast."

Demyan Parkinson puts forward for that era the bold theory

that time practically does not exist. Only after more than a hundred years will the English physicist Julian Barbour publish a similar theory and become the subject of ridicule by his colleagues. Just as, instead of his son, Lavrentiy Parkinson was ridiculed by physicists of the time. In short, our hero believes that only the present is real, and only conditionally, while the past and the future are purely grammatical categories, projections of memories and expectations. The *present* moment owes its elusiveness to its oscillatory nature. Because, according to Parkinson, *now* possesses a certain reality thanks to the "penetrations" of the Divine energies, but at the same time it has no true duration because those particles penetrate into *nothing*. If we apply this teaching to quantum mechanics, which should be published soon, "quanta" are nothing but a particle of time, and overall existence can be defined as ***nothing*** *that has a certain duration*.

After an introductory chapter that has some connection with what is called science, Parkinson's study turns to the mystery, more precisely the mysticism of Genesis. We note that Charles Darwin's famous work on *the origin of species* had already been published and that Moscow intellectuals, always hungry for simplification and innovation, are always ready to turn into animals, read it carefully during the day and keep it under their pillows at night. In that fascination with the animal world, in that joyful acceptance of the finality of death, Parkinson sees a reliable sign of the coming of the end times. And he's absolutely right. Only one letter separates evolution from revolution. He, of course, has no illusions that his writings can change anything; his work is rather a kind of personal Jacob's ladder, which he climbs in an attempt to escape from himself. As a part of that project, one should certainly consider the exhaustive essay *Dislocation of Temptations*, from which, unfortunately, only fragments have been preserved. The review was published under the pseudonym Joakim Ernestovich Gromeko-Baljberg, causing scandal and considerable confusion in the cultural community at the time due to the fact that one Joakim Ernestovich Gromeko-Baljberg was in the Tver province, who—flattered and insulted at the same time—sued the printer Vsevolodov, demanding a huge author's fee.[15] J. E. Gromeko-Baljberg won the lawsuit[16] and even gained some fame in the obscure circles of pseudo-mysticism. No wonder, if we consider the original conception of the essay by which D. A. tries to make a synthesis of Plato's myth and the Old Testament story. Here we come across a spherical Adam (Plato's influence), but such an Adam is not an ordinary ball, a sphere filled with flesh and entrails, but rather its structure is complex: it consists of seven concentric spheres rotating within each other, in perfect harmony with the seven celestial spheres of the macrocosm. Starting from the thesis that the spiritual precedes the material, Parkinson describes the outer sphere as the place where Adam's personality and the sefira *Malkuth* merge; the sphere below it represents Eden, where the next rotating sphere is inhabited by the material Adam. Then follow the spheres of ideas about creatures and things, and finally, as the last circle, the planet Earth itself, which Adam contains and inhabits at the same time. (The idea of verticality in which all things are inextricably linked by interpenetration, the eternal obsession of Demyan Parkinson, is presented in a brilliant way.) Now we come

15. That it is impossible in Russia to come up with non-existent names and surnames is proven by F. M. Dostoyevsky. He really tried to conjure up the most absurd names for his protagonists only to find out that, in the vast spaces of the Empire, there are people, actually more of them, who have those very names.

16. It remains unknown how D. A. managed to gather the money to pay off the namesake of his own fiction.

to the mystery of the Fall. According to Parkinson, *Creation* was not a final act but the beginning of an endless process in which the *created* through Adam's activity is elevated into the *uncreated*. The world immediately after Genesis still contains a high percentage of nothingness. In order for the instability of such a state to prevail, Parkinson believes (and here we see the influence of St. Maximus the Confessor), the descent and incarnation of the Son was inevitable, even if the Fall did not happen. (One cannot leave such a task to a man even when he is seemingly perfect.)

In the pages that follow, Demyan Parkinson, alias Gromeko-Baljberg, presents a fabulous theory about tasting the fruit of the *Tree of the Knowledge of Good and Evil*. "Quite contrary to today's understanding of eating," says one of the surviving fragments, "which turns into a source of unworthy pleasure, even in the times immediately after the Fall, eating was the arduous task of transforming (transmuting) what was eaten into oneself. It is in that sense that one should also understand the parable of Adam's tasting of the fruit from the *Tree of the Knowledge of Good and Evil*. Adam was to eat that fruit, but not before he tasted the fruit from the *Tree of Life*; that is, not before everything is imbued with life, which could not be achieved by personal effort, his success, but only by the descent of the second person of the Trinity. He, therefore, wants to *know* life before he has acquired it, and with that desire he brings pride and impatience into himself (and into all his descendants), is cast out of Paradise, prevented from eating from the *Tree of Life*, and subjected to death as an imperfect life in which are concealed the endless possibilities of corruption so they would not be perpetuated." What happened further?

"Adam ate from the *Tree of the Knowledge of Good and Evil*, digested what he ate, turned it into his body, and now he realized that his greatness and his radiance deprived of divine support are only darkness and dust. He learns that he himself is both good and evil. The most common possibility. And not just that! The harmony of the spheres is disturbed; they collapse, and Adam, who until recently was the master of the Earth and all creatures, is chained by matter and exposed to its elements."

The fact that only a few fragments of the extensive review, despite three editions in enviable print runs, remain available, is a reliable sign that Demyan Parkinson entered the Garden of Forbidden Knowledge. Unlike the ungodly writings, which became more and more extensive over time, his reputation was doomed to gradual disappearance. Thus, attempting to reconstruct Adam's fall, Demyan Lavrentyevich Parkinson cleared the way to his own fall—the inevitable punishment for all who dare to reveal that which is to remain hidden. The punishment did not go unnoticed by the vain and greedy Gromeko-Baljberg, who was covered with Old Testament ulcers for which the medicine of that time had no cure, and his property was devastated by a plague of locusts. But the punishment for the real author of the text is in a way even worse.

The punishment is no less and no more—Lou Salome.

It is not certain whether Lou Salome came to Mitrofanovsk before or after the victorious campaign against Italy and, later, Europe. The mechanisms for determining the chronology in her case do not work; she possesses an ominous energy charge that deforms the space-time lattice. Which, more precisely, deforms everything that is in its vicinity. It is true that all women hide their age, but Lou has no measure. It will be noted that she was born in 1861, although the books of those born in St. Petersburg indicate another date with paper fingers: February 12, 1831. So, at a time when she was attracted to the legendary Sodom events in the Parkinson's summer house, she came to

Mitrofanovsk—a time which we cannot determine precisely for the reasons mentioned—she is already a mature woman, experienced in all perversions, so imbued with debauchery of all kinds that she looks (and so she is portrayed) like a virgin. Immediately upon arrival, she casts an eye on young D. A., intuitively feeling that this is a great man, a species she cannot resist. D. A. actually has only one drawback: he has no money. It turns out, however, that this shortcoming will save his life. "I learned more about hell from Lou than from reading all the church fathers," Parkinson confided to a friend many years later. We don't know what kind of hell that is. As always, when it comes to Lou, everything takes place behind closed doors. The only evidence is the inhuman screams occasionally heard from Demyan's chambers. D. A. himself is reluctant to talk about it. Only from time to time does he reveal something to one of his closest friends. But he writes nothing down. A few of his friends do, however. In P. A. Vronsky's diary, for example, we come across a note that is hard to believe:

> [. . .] when we retired to the salon after dinner, Demyan told me that he had witnessed a monstrous event that day. Namely, he had gone to the post office on some business, and when he returned, he heard Lou giving orders to the servants in a rough, somewhat altered voice. Unsuspecting, he entered the room and found Lou, completely naked, with her mouth full of sweets, at the same time speaking from her anus. "To make matters worse," Parkinson told me, "my arrival didn't upset her at all. She turned, laughed, and tweeted from the same improper place: my dear, you've been gone quite a while."

Now the character of the witch Hildegard (who also spoke

from her buttocks) from the apocryphal tale of the last days of Jakob Böhme is somewhat clearer. Although due to the pre-revolutionary confusion in the chronology, it is still not clear whether the apocrypha was written before or after Salome's stay in Mitrofanovsk.[17] In any case, Demyan Parkinson realized in time that his connection with Lou was leading him to ruin. What else to expect from a woman who thinks that people should be fitted with some kind of instrument panel with indicators that show body temperature, walking speed, blood pressure, pulse, hydration level in the body, and even mood? It is the nineteenth century of great discoveries, but even the most ardent advocates of the mechanization of all and everything do not go that far. Demyan Parkinson pretended to be poorer than he was; he could only offer his beloved books, among them one of the first translations of Friedrich Nietzsche. Which proved fatal to the German philosopher. After just reading a few sentences, Lou realized that Nietzsche is something completely different. Something that she needs: he despises any mysticism, he is extroverted; at the same time, he knows the most influential European artists and goes to ballrooms, so different from the half-ruined salons in the Parkinson's house, which, above all, smell of dried fish and borscht. And one morning, Lou Salome leaves Mitrofanovsk

---

17. Concerning the chronological chaos at the end of the nineteenth century, it seems incomprehensible to the modern reader; this arises from the fact that the dramatic events of the period were classified and arranged, later, but not always in the correct order. Ultimately, if that chaos had not existed, there would have been no revolution which, among other things, could have been avoided if the Tsar had heeded the advice of Arhonotovich's friend, Count Vronsky, who was trying to convince him to do away with the month of October 1918 by decree, and to make up for it by having an additional October the next year. Instead of listening to the counsel that would have saved both his head and his empire, Nikolai II ordered that Vronsky be sent to an insane asylum.

on a velocipede, leaving terrible devastation in Demyan Parkinson's soul, the probable cause of his later misogyny and strict celibacy.

Her departure accelerates the development of events. The landowners in Moscow have finally sobered up, are sending dispatches to the managers of the estates around Mitrofanovsk, demanding money and receiving notifications in disbelief that their estates have been sold off and have long since been laid to waste. That, in fact, due to the bad calculation of drunken surveyors who convert versts into kilometers, these properties no longer exist. That Mitrofanovsk is no more. There are no surrounding hamlets. There is no river Psary. That all this is now hundreds of damn miles away in China or Manchuria. All the same, Lavrentiy Parkinson is still condemned to prison. He is sentenced to exile in Siberia, which he deeply desires. (There, in a completely Russian style, he would finally sober up, repent, and spend his last years in incessant prayers.) However, before we continue the story of his son, we stop for a moment in Moscow to attend the procession of convicts, including Lavrentiy Akakyevich, on a train that will take them to some snowbound backwater. Among the gathered folk, in the midst of shouts, insults and occasional merciful remarks, we see Fyodor Mikhailovich (he does not miss such opportunities in his search for inspiration); "Fyodor Mikhailovich, Fyodor Mikhailovich!" shouts Lavrentiy Parkinson from the line, chained in shackles. The writer of the *Karamazovs* takes out his notebook for a moment, but immediately returns it to his pocket. He casts a contemptuous glance at his former host and patron, turns his head away and pretends not to know him. The great pervert Parkinson goes to Siberia with the bitter knowledge that Dostoyevsky will never dedicate even the most meager sentence to him, such as: "In the line of prisoners, L. A. Parkinson was also present, the former landowner who drank away his own property, and that of several neighbors."

Demyan had no choice. He had to leave Mitrofanovsk. Entering the train, he looked back at his birthplace for the last time and saw that the magic of ecstasy, the endless drunkenness, and orgies, had dissipated; Mitrofanovsk had dawned in its ruggedness of muddy streets, neglected houses, and even more neglected residents. Now he understands Fyodor Mikhailovich to some extent; such a city—if it is a city—could in no way fit into the urban plan of his novels. Indeed, if we take a closer look, despite the pronounced social tones, Dostoyevsky places the action of his books mainly in St. Petersburg, Moscow, or some fashionable spa in Europe. He never writes about places where there are no casinos. Parkinson, therefore, got on a train and traveled into a ten-year exile into the unknown. What did he do those ten years? Where did he live? Whereabouts did he wander? We will never know any of that. Moreover, we don't even know if he was in Russia at all. To make things more complicated—he himself remembered nothing of the time. Or did not want to remember. It was not until 1901 that we stumbled upon him quite by accident on the bustling streets of Laleli, a shopping district in Istanbul.

Also, not without some surprise, we learn that D.A. was the owner of the elegant boarding house Karadeniz, which specialized in accommodating romantic and tuberculous Russian countesses who, tucked into cashmere blankets, spent their last days comfortably watching the sunset on the Bosporus from the balcony. And that is, in brief, all that can be found out. No matter how extensive our research is, the traces lead just to the Russian-Turkish border. From that point onward, hotels would leave a heavy stamp on the life of our hero: he would either run them or live in them.

Running a hotel, however, does not stop him from writing apocryphal books. He enriches his non-existent and increasingly extensive bibliography with the work *Tractatus antiheliocentricus,* from the title of which it is easy to guess the topic. This time he was more careful. Authorship is now attributed to *Michael Sendivogius,* a seventeenth-century alchemist, on whom he draws the hood of astronomers, sworn opponents of Nicolaus Copernicus and other proponents of the "resurrected pagan cult of the Sun," as he describes them in the *Preface* by the ostensible Leipzig professor Von Klosowski. To fully insure against any possibility of the book being attributed to him, Parkinson backdates the year of publication (1799), and perfectly matches the graphic equipment and binding to the alleged time of printing, all with the anagram *Divi leschi genus amo,* which contains all the letters of the fictional author's name.

What, then, is this writing about, which takes on the heliocentric model of the universe—one of the foundations of European rationalism? In short (the space of this text does not allow extensive analysis), Demyan Parkinson sees heliocentrism as the insidious abolition of monotheism and its replacement by the ancient cult of the Sun. The violent relocation of the Earth from the center of the universe to its extreme periphery has no practical significance. Maritime navigation continues to operate with the Earth as a focal point. Not without irony, Parkinson, alias *Sendivogius,* invites proponents of the doctrine to embark on a cruise on a ship whose helmsman would determine the course based on the newly introduced position of the Earth. "That theory," he writes in one chapter, "does not introduce any *order* into celestial mechanics, because it is falsely portrayed. On the contrary: the celestial bodies remain in number and in their places. Instead, disorder is introduced into the spirits of people and from there spreads through unexplored spaces of the microcosm into higher spheres. After all, the Earth does not owe its central place to its position in space, but to Adam, as the center of Creation. After all, in order to determine the center, it is necessary to have a clearly defined periphery, which we do not have in this case. In an undefined system filled with billions of objects, it is absolutely impossible to determine where everything is." Demyan Parkinson supports his bold thesis with earthquake statistics, which show a dramatic increase in seismic earthquakes since the adoption of the doctrine of heliocentrism to the present day.[18]

Inspired pages follow where our hero elaborates on the further sinister implications of heliocentrism. Due to the disturbances created in the subtle hierarchy of celestial mechanics, social disruptions occur, which are reflected in the decreasing readiness of the human masses to submit to any idea of a higher order, symbolized in the principle of monarchy. When the Earth is not at the center of the world, individual personalities become the center. And soon this confusion leads to the occasional application of written codes of absurd "human rights." Many a naïve king, dedicated to the welfare of his subjects, happily accepts "scientific truth" in order to soon find himself in the midst of the roar of a crowd taking him to the guillotine or the gallows.

As we said: the fraud was discovered thanks to earthquake statistics which D. A. inadvertently extended for a hundred years after the death of the alleged author *Sendivogius*. The Apocrypha is unmasked. But Demyan Parkinson is not. He is now, in fact, a subject of the Ottoman Empire, a hotelier named İsmail Ağa Çengi.

18. A mistake hard to understand by the otherwise proverbially cautious Demyan Arhotovich. The statistics he offered in the study included earthquakes all the way up to 1900, which served sometime later to reveal his authorship, since the year of publication for the book is stated as 1799.

The poisonous arrows of rationalist critics hit the heart of a fictional Turk, a citizen of the rotten eastern empire, from whom nothing smarter can be expected. Although his real name has remained unsullied, Demyan Parkinson finds it very difficult to endure vicious attacks, which to some extent justifies the poisonous tongues that think the propensity for apocryphalness in our hero is owed more to vanity than the love of anonymity. However, from İsmail Ağa Çengi to Demyan Parkinson is only one step, many are ready to take it, and that is why he decides to change his formal identity again. Overnight, he sells the boarding house *Karadeniz,* leaves the bereaved countesses to the oriental whims of the new owner, and heads off in an unknown direction. Just in case, he has no name for a while. But he does not rest. He drops the pseudonym İsmail Ağa, but not his pen. Somewhere in the backwaters of Anatolia—subsequent analyses have established that the paper originates from the area of Trabzon—he writes the second part of the *Tractatus antiheliocentricus,* in which he justifies the missing İsmail Ağa Çengi. The modest Aga, he claims, resorted to attributing authorship to another man because of prejudices about Turkish philosophers in the European public. His name alone on the cover of the book would be enough to dismiss its contents as nonsense. Proponents of geocentrism, after all, face such a fate even if they bear much more acceptable names to the European ear. But he does not give up on the theses presented in the book.

The Earth, he claims, is still at the center of creation.

The Sun is just heating and lighting.

Where was Demyan Parkinson hiding all that time? Where everyone else goes who for some reason wants to get away from the public—in the army. Armies don't pay much attention to biographies and identities anyway; according to von Clausewitz, the ideal soldier should only have a surface. Both in terms of strategy and in terms of tactics, only the surface is usable. What should a general do with nonsense like "inner life" or "personality"? The fact that a living being was needed to fill a uniform, helmet, boots, and make a weapon mobile and deadly is only a concession to the imperfections of war technology; the weakest element of the military machinery which, due to its weakness, usually has to change. Each subjectivity and peculiarity further shortens the working life and usability of that variable element which, although it is the least valuable, should be nourished and treated in addition. In the Ottoman army, that approach was brought to perfection. There, the *asker* doesn't even have a number. (What would be the purpose of numbering soldiers in an army in which officers below the rank of major do not know how to count at all?) That is why the numerical condition is determined by approximation. According to the density of the battle unit. It is understandable that such a place perfectly suited the needs of Demyan Parkinson. Cruel discipline, frequent floggings, sleeping on the bare ground, horrible Anatolian frosts, all this our hero accepts as obstacles on the ladder of spiritual success. "One must suffer. Until we tame, or, better yet, kill the animal within us, we will not be able to be human," notes DA in a letter to young René Guénon. And in the continuation, he adds visionary-like: "But in our time, the refined art of suffering is no longer appreciated. On the contrary: there seems to be a huge effort to avoid it at all costs. Just look at the shameless rise of the pharmaceutical industry. The sad flourishing of private medical practices. And the depths to which we have sunk will be completely clear to you. There is no nonsense that is not considered worthy of hospital treatment, and I am afraid that this subversive practice will soon become a right; that, moreover, this shameless parasitism will be financed by the states themselves, thus paving the way for their own downfall. How different is it from the sober understanding expressed in Plato's *Republic*, according to which medical skill should be used exclusively to treat perfectly healthy people who in some cases cut themselves, break their arms or catch a cold, while the sick and weak should be left to fate: either to their own strength to be healed, or to die more or less cleansed by suffering and pain. I dare to predict that this unworthy right will be used even by officers; that even this caste, once ranked just behind brahmins and philosophers, will visit doctors' offices and laboratories, urinate in ridiculous vessels, and anxiously await the results. That is how far the degeneration processes will lead. If it can be accepted that farmers, clerks, and workers are ill, the practice of officers' sick leave is absolutely unacceptable. The state of being ill is in sharp contradiction with the very essence of that profession.

Who needs sick officers at all?"

This vision gains value if we remember that at the time when Demyan Parkinson joined the Ottoman army, it was still unthinkable for an officer to be ill. Sickness in the ordinary ranks is also looked down upon with disdain. Such people are burdened with the most difficult duties and assigned the most dangerous tasks. Platonism as a practice of the Ottoman army? Strange but true. If it were not so, would the Porta have ruled over half the world for centuries? If an officer—as was the case with Major Kemal Paşa Mustafa, the later "Father of Turkey," who secretly suffered from cirrhosis of the liver—accidentally falls ill, then officer's honor orders him to cover it up, to treat himself and fight because, if he is unable to cope with his own pain, how could one expect him to defeat a superior enemy on the battlefield? Kemal Paşa, to whom our hero D. A. was stronger at the time, did so. His personal pharmacy is militarily neat and extremely modest, and consists of several *hoca* incantations, mint tea, and snuff.

Providence itself, though in a somewhat strange way, seems to unite the two visionaries. Between Kemal Paşa and Demyan Parkinson, despite the insurmountable difference in rank during that time, a sincere (and long-lasting) friendship is born. Which in no way relieves our hero of the duty of cleaning boots, washing the major's clothes, cooking and seducing easy girls, filling and cleaning pipes with opium—duties that, it must be said, Demyan Parkinson performs extremely conscientiously. "If you are not able," he will note somewhere, "to serve a superior officer with perfect devotion, how do you expect to serve the Lord with steadfastness?"

Kemal Paşa, however, is not what he seems to be; fornication with Circassian prostitutes, smoking opium, immoderate enjoyment of plenty of food and sweets—all this is the fate of oriental scenography, the curse of the East, beneath which hides an extremely educated and intelligent person. In hours of enjoyment, Kemal Paşa invites Demyan Parkinson to his tent. (When he is especially in a good mood, he allows him to sleep there, curled up next to his bed; otherwise D.A. sleeps on an asura in front of his tent. Or perhaps it is more accurate to say—a chador) Along with tea and a narghile, the two of them hold endless discussions about art, philosophy, and religion. Kemal Paşa cannot sleep (he is tormented by his liver and a bad conscience); Demyan Parkinson, on the other hand, happily accepts any occasion to avoid the softness of surrendering to sleep. Here's how, if you believe the reconstruction of one of the mysteries of Demyan Parkinson, those discussions are going on. "Well, Aziz," (Aziz was Parkinson's provisional name at the time), "if you already like to write, why do you avoid signing with your own name what you write? Are you afraid of taking responsibility?" "No!" Aziz, that is Parkinson, answered. "It is impossible to avoid responsibility by changing your name. But writing is quite a sensitive thing. It is giving shape to your internal chaos. In doing so, you shouldn't get your own name involved. *The name is the house of the being.* (If the reconstruction is correct, then what is suspected is evident: French intellectuals gladly and frequently "borrow" from our hero.) And the house must not be filled with dubious furniture. It would be best if books were published only with titles, without the names of the authors, but such books do not sell." Kemal Paşa takes a deep fragrant drag from the narghile (stage directions are unavoidable also in reconstructions) and says, "Evet! [Turkish: 'yes.'] This world has truly fallen low. I wonder: can we go on? The maintenance of the cosmic order has fallen on the shoulders of the military and police guilds, and this is not their intended job. We, the soldiers and the *seymens* (here he rose slightly on the couch), are the last defenders of the idea of the center; in fact, we are sad Don Quixotes charging at the windmills of impending chaos. And for that excruciating service, instead of gratitude, we receive contempt. And accusations of cruelty and genocide. And even all that cruelty is not able to establish a more or less stable state of things. You were absolutely right in that text of yours. What was it called? *Corpus Hermeticum.* The chaos in the word is a consequence of understanding that the Earth is not the center of the universe. And now, out you go, to the asura, I want to read some Nietzsche . . ."

"Wait!" Kemal Paşa stops him halfway through that short journey. "There's one more thing. Abortions! You forgot about abortions. If you print another edition one day, be sure to mention them. Satan ensures that those who would be born as the strongest and smartest be aborted. And Allah allows it in order to punish this generation."

Reading these lines, no matter how much we doubted their credibility, we cannot escape the impression that Kemal Paşa and his adjutant are completely right. Because the two of them, in the middle of a desert of even more dubious credibility, exposed to a possible attack by one of the countless rebel hordes that roam Anatolia, spend time talking about the so-called last things, while the learned heads, the elite of this world, in comfortable and warm clubs lead banal discussions about price increases, cricket matches, and love affairs. But the structure of the world is as follows: all big things, regardless of the value of their first sign, are conceived in inconspicuous places: the Buddha attains enlightenment in a remote forest; Jesus is born in a barn; Hitler acquires his first supporters in obscure Munich beer halls. Kemal Paşa, later Atatürk, shaped the idea of reforming the Ottoman Empire in a military camp, using an ammunition box instead of a desk. Which proves to be an extremely practical solution, because some of Paşa's ideas are, so to speak, shot into the resentful conscience with bullets from that box. In the major's law code, everything is militarily meticulous, already foreseen down to the smallest detail: the ban on fezzes and veils; the secularization of Turkey; genocides to be carried out for the purpose of complete Turkification[19] (together with the dates of the pogroms and a list of the names of those to be killed); and finally, a project that Kemal Paşa introduced into his vision at the ingenious persuasion of Demyan Parkinson: the reform of the Turkish alphabet and language (as D.A.'s first covert influence on the world historical process).

The stubborn Atatürk does not easily renounce the

19. In the sense of the functionality of the national state, Kemal Atatürk was completely right, despite the fact that his vision did not fit into the framework of the newly arisen doctrines of political correctness and human rights, because such a state can function only under the condition that it is inhabited by only one nation.

oriental seduction of the Arabic alphabet. However, as time passes, Parkinson's arguments are increasingly irrefutable and Paşa finally agrees to the reform, provided that Parkinson renounces his authorship and commits himself to lifelong silence, which he gladly accepts. And he keeps his word. His lips are sealed. But sometimes, especially when he drinks one or two, Kemal Paşa loosens his tongue in front of his mistresses. In the world of high politics, again, every second or third mistress is a spy of some foreign power, and thanks to that fact we have a transcript of one of Atatürk's monologues, taken from the archives of a secret service whose name, understandably, we must not mention:

[The preceding sentences are crossed out in black ink and completely illegible.] ". . . yes, yes, Aziz Parkinson is crucial for the decision to abolish the use of the Arabic alphabet by decree. But, don't tell a soul about this! Did you hear? At first, I did not intend to get mixed up with linguistics. I thought that, in politics, the alphabet was of no importance. After all, it shouldn't be. But that damn Russian showed me that it really is. 'Kemal Paşa,' he would say, scrubbing his boots or polishing his sword, 'the character of a nation is destined to be determined by their alphabet. Here's an example: The Chinese! They are an eternal puzzle for us for the simple reason that we do not understand their ideograms. In ancient times, the eyes of the Chinese were like ours; with the introduction of letters, they slowly become slanted due to constant visual contact with the curvy lines of the writing brush. Take a look at any Chinese ideogram and everything will be immediately clear. There's one more thing: pictorial writing conserves meaning. True, spoken language changes like all others, but traditional meanings are locked in the hard safes of ideograms and there is no linguistic aberration that can disrupt them, which gives this nation perseverance despite (or thanks to) constant changes and unity regardless of the endless diversity of dialects. Even the Great Wall itself is nothing but a huge ideogram, the meaning of which some experts translate as: barbarians, stop here! And that, thanks to the enormity of the ideogram, worked. The barbarians obediently stopped at its foot. The Great Wall, as you know, never had military reinforcement . . .

"My love, please, pour me a *yeni rakı* . . .

"Where was I? Yes! What objection could I make to such an argument? It's true, I read somewhere myself: The Great Wall did not have military reinforcement, only the mean-spirited writer of the book attributed it to the alleged decadence of the Chinese empire. Utter nonsense! Decadence is impossible in China for the simple reason that they cut down any progress at the root. At that very moment, a brilliant idea flashed in my mind: perhaps I, too, should build a Great Wall that would surround Turkey? But a number of obstacles immediately arose. Written in Arabic script, with all its curves and hooks, it also comes loaded with a long list of enemies that should be deterred, the wall would not only be too expensive but would cover the entire surface of Turkey. In the military sense, that is not a bad solution at all: the ideal defense is the fortification of every inch of what is being defended. But Turkey, despite everything I have done for it, is not an ideal country and cannot claim the right to an ideal defense.

"Aziz, I must admit, was very persistent.

"Day after day, hour after hour, he continued to convince me of the benefits of changing the alphabet. I asked myself: is the well-being of Turkey so close to his heart, or is there a desire to contribute to something great, while remaining anonymous, and thus be free of any responsibility if something goes wrong? Who knows? But his arguments were undeniable. I remember that as if it were yesterday:

Aziz, next to a brazier, is making tea. And he says, 'Kemal-aga, the influence of writing on a nation greatly exceeds the limits of literacy and permeates every pore of a community. The use of Arabic scripts in itself arouses in men a desire to dress in accordance with the morphology of alephs and dalets; it simply cries out for wearing baggy pants, turbans, pointy-toed shoes and slippers . . . In short, everything that forbids access to Europe and its luxurious salons. Don't get me wrong, but Europeanism consists of little other than the European way of dressing, which in Istanbul is still mockingly called *alafranga*—"like the Frenchies." I know you intend to change that. But think about it a little! If you ban turbans, fezzes, and veils, and the Arabic alphabet remains in use, you will then face a series of armed rebellions resulting from the discrepancy between the way you dress and the way you write. To make the clothing reform successful, you need to reform the alphabet and introduce Cyrillic instead of Arabic letters.'

"So, Cyrillic! That's what Aziz was aiming for! I immediately recognized the tentacles of Great Russian imperialism in that proposal. Too many in the Ottoman Empire used that alphabet. We had very bad experiences with Cyrillic. I wondered: is Aziz a Russian agent? And I immediately rejected that possibility. He wasn't any kind of agent. But the Russians are like that: they always work for the benefit of Greater Russia, even when they don't want to or when they are not aware of it at all. The use of Russian Cyrillic was not impossible. The sound "I," for example, could easily be replaced with "bI." "C," it would be harder with it, but I could, if I were crazy, borrow "Ђ" from the Serbs. If I had done so, if I had introduced Russian Cyrillic, not even fifty years would have passed, and the Turks would have turned into Russians. There are no big differences between them anyway.

"I did not want to offend Aziz. Even less to punish him. He was an inexhaustible mine of useful ideas. That's why I resorted to oriental cunning. 'You're right, Aziz,' I told him, 'you just forget that the Russian alphabet isn't looked upon very well in Europe either. So, I will meet your idea half-way: I will abolish the Arabic alphabet, and introduce the Latin instead.' 'As you wish, Kemal-aga', Aziz said sullenly, 'just so you know, Turkey will soon become a Catholic country. And here's why . . .'" [The rest of the report is also crossed out in black ink.]

The reform of the Turkish alphabet is still in the phase of fantasy, which, when he wakes up from his opium dreams, Kemal Paşa does not believe either. How unrealistic all this is, is shown by the fact that he himself did not know the Latin alphabet at that time. Yes, he reads Nietzsche, but it is the Russian edition put out by *Voznesensky and Son*. The most unbridled fantasies, however, almost always find their way to the surface of reality (this is important for the further course of the story about D. A.), while at the same time the most rationally based projects usually end in chaos and nothingness. One morning, Demyan Parkinson signed a contract (drawn up in Arabic!!!) which waives the copyright on the idea of alphabet reform. In return, he received a discharge from the army, a bag of ducats, a *hoca* incantation against spells, and a somewhat inconspicuous place in the Turkish diplomatic service (*birinci katip*, First Secretary), which, for now, is adorned with a footnote: *When Kemal Paşa comes to power*. We see them briefly as they part, at a crowded Anatolian train station whose name we cannot read because it is (still) written in Arabic. The very next moment, they suddenly disappear in the opaque cloud of a sandstorm, which after a while moves on further north.

We no longer see Atatürk, Parkinson, or the train station. In that God forbidden place, all traces of Demyan Lavrentyevich are lost. I never heard anything about him again, but as an experienced observer of world events here and there, I recognized in some event his invisible handwriting, and the visible influences of the refined disease that took its name from him.

Demyan Lavrentyevich Parkinson, the inventor of the horrible disease, died of exhaustion in 1947 under the false name of Nikolai Nikolayevich Kuznetsov, in a gulag on the River Kolyma. Until that day, he tried to change the environment from the perspective of a strange disease, composing fragments of a long since broken, integral picture of the world, in constant struggle with the chimeras of true disease and false health and their inverted roles as the infernal backbones of the world in revolutions, wars, esotericism, and alchemy.

This book is a novel which is sometimes a history, and a history which is sometimes a novel. The boundary between genres, and truth and lies, can only be determined by a brave reader.

Translator's Note

While Svetislav Basara is certainly one of Serbia's most prominent writers, he is by no means a favorite son among the country's literary and intellectual elite. His wide-ranging historical, philosophical, and political expositions often defy the everyday maxims about the society's struggle to become a modern European entity. His voice could be received as inspiring and innovative, yet it is often met with disgruntled responses from ideologues, historical revisionists, and would-be authoritarians. His writing style(s) show a distinct disdain for the bedrock of much of modern Serbian literature: the historical narrative as a platform for the patriotic program and the further magnification of the greatness of the nation. *The Rise and Fall of Parkinson's Disease* pans out from that environment and thereby offers the world reader a broader view that captures the ills of Western Civilization.

To present that horizon to the reader, Basara employs a number of devices to trigger the reader's recollection, to encourage the audience to reflect further, to question longstanding clichés, and to raise consciousness of unjustified beliefs in traditional "values". In 2025, as we watch Western society and other parts of the world swirl into seeming madness, we tend to ask the question: how did we get here? The "rise and fall" in the title harkens back to Gibbon's classic work on the Roman Empire, and Basara is broadening that scope for us to include our very own civilization. In order to do so, he resources his usual blend of historical narrative and meta-fiction, pseudo-sourcing, philosophical tractates, parody, and even spices it all with a little burlesque.

Our ever-growing obsession with personal health, diet, and disease mitigation has recently caught stride with our ancient and lingering fascination with the spiritual and ethereal. Thus, *The Rise and Fall of Parkinson's Disease* is a timely contribution to the definitions of physical, mental, and spiritual (or moral?) health as we explore the dimensions of *well-being.*

Basara uses a wide range of stylistic, syntactic and lexical devices that ought to be expressed by their corresponding forms in a different language. If one adds to that the extensive number of historical and literary references, including the usual problems of register and lexical precision, the challenge confronting the translator becomes quite clear. Hopefully, that challenge has been met in this rendition of his text. All shortcomings in the result are most certainly mine.

Randall A. Major
Novi Sad, Serbia
May 2025

Born in 1953, **Svetislav Basara** is a major figure in Serbian and Eastern European literature. The author of more than twenty novels, essay and short story collections, he is also the winner of numerous awards and honors, including the NIN Prize in 2008. Between 2001 and 2005 Basara served as Serbia and Montenegro's ambassador to Cyprus.

Randall A. Major is a linguist and translator. He taught in the English department at the University of Novi Sad, and was one of the editors and translators of the Serbian Prose in Translation series produced by Geopoetika Publishing in Belgrade. His translations of Basara's *In Search of the Grail* and *Fata Morgana* are also available from Dalkey Archive Press.

www.ingramcontent.com/pod-product-compliance
Lightning Source LLC
Jackson TN
JSHW022036090226
97357JS00001B/1